# The New Girl

Shifter Academy: United #1

Scarlett Haven

# Thursday, August 20
# Shifter Academy.

My hand shakes as I open up the large manila envelope. My name is printed on the front. Layla Rosewood. I never get any mail. Come to think of it, I don't think I've ever had anything mailed to me before.

*Shifter Academy*, the return address reads.

Why would I get anything from Shifter Academy?

I am a shifter, but I've never been allowed to attend Shifter Academy. Alpha George won't let me. He says I'm too weak, and that I would make the other panthers look bad.

I'm the runt of my pride. In my human form, I barely stand over five feet tall. It's no surprise that my panther is also tiny. Alpha George is embarrassed by how small I am, and I can hardly blame him. I *would* make the pride look bad to the other shifters.

I am eighteen now, and I'm about to start my senior year of high school. I'm homeschooled. Just because I'm not permitted to attend Shifter Academy doesn't mean they'd let me go to a public high school. We're not allowed to associate with the humans at all, so a couple women from the pack teach those of us who are either too young or too weak for Shifter Academy.

Still, the envelope that I hold gives me hope.

Maybe I really can go to Shifter Academy.

I've dreamed of going my whole life. Most everybody from the pride goes.

I wonder if I should take the piece of mail to Alpha George, but curiosity gets the better of me. I rip open the envelope and pull out the letter.

*Dear Layla Rosewood,*

*It has come to our attention that despite being of high school age, you are not on the enrollment at Shifter Academy. As you may or may not know, Shifter Academy is mandatory for all young shifters. Your alpha has been notified of the error, and you are expected to be in attendance on Monday, August 24. Please be sure to arrive early so you may have the chance to get settled before classes begin.*

*While we are very thrilled to have you join us, know that failure to attend will not only have bad consequences for you, but also for your pride and your alpha.*

*Thank you for your cooperation.*

*Sincerely,*
*Margot Westwood*
*Dean of Shifter Academy*
*Wolf Shifter*

I am in complete shock as I read over the letter addressed to me.

I double check the name on the front, then I triple check it.

This has got to be some kind of mistake, right? Alpha George doesn't want me going to school there.

Still, hope floods me at the thought of attending for my senior year.

With the letter in hand, I run up the steps toward my house. I'm about to throw open the front door when I remember that Dad is probably asleep. A quick glance at the time on my phone reveals that it's just after three in the afternoon. It's best not to wake him up before dinner.

Still, I smile when I look at the letter in my hand. There is a handbook inside with the rules, dress code, and my classroom schedule. I pull out the book and begin to read.

I'm really going to Shifter Academy.

It's truly happening!

A little later that afternoon, as I'm cooking dinner, somebody rings the doorbell. I cringe, hoping whoever it is didn't wake up my father. He was out late last night, and he will be very upset if he is woken up.

I run toward the door and open it before they can ring the doorbell twice, and I'm shocked to see Alpha George standing on the other side.

Alpha George never comes to visit.

"Hello, Alpha." I bow to him, just as he has asked everybody in the pride to do out of respect. "Please, come in. I am cooking dinner if you want some."

He walks inside, but his nose is wrinkled in disgust. "I'm not interested in any food you have to offer me, you filthy runt."

For whatever reason, my alpha has never been fond of me. I know it's because I'm small and weak. He thinks I am a burden to our pride. He's right. I'm not able to fight like others. But I try to pull my weight in other ways. It's never enough, though.

The door to my father's room opens with a thunk. He walks out, his footsteps heavy, and I cringe.

Alpha George definitely woke up my father, and I know my dad will be taking it out on me as soon as Alpha leaves.

I shut the door behind Alpha as he strides farther into the house.

"Alpha." Dad bows to greet him, much like I did. "What did we do to deserve the honor of you graciously coming to our home?"

Alpha's eyes are hard as he turns to glare at my father. "Shifter Academy found out about Layla, and the council is on my ass to send her to school there for senior year."

Dad looks between Alpha and me. "Certainly there is something we can do about it."

"No." Alpha's voice is hard as he looks at me. "Pack a bag and get to Shifter Academy. But you better not embarrass the pride. One wrong move, and you will be out on the streets."

My bottom lip trembles at his threat.

Alpha often threatens to kick me out of the pride, saying he doesn't need a runt like me. But this time, I truly think he means it.

Alpha George turns and leaves the house, slamming the door shut behind him. The entire wall rattles at the force.

Dad turns his attention to me, his eyes narrowing. "What did you do?"

"N-n-nothing," I stutter, reaching over to grab the envelope from the counter. "I just got this today."

Dad grabs the letter from my hand forcefully, scanning over it.

"This was your doing," he accuses.

I shake my head. "N-no. I s-s-swear."

He throws down the paper and takes a step toward me. He pulls his hand back, smacking me across the face, hitting me with enough force that I'm thrown back against the wall. My vision goes black for a second, and my back hits the wall so hard that it knocks the breath out of me and I fall onto my knees on the ground.

"You better do as Alpha George said. I better not see you here again."

"Y-yes, s-si-s-sir." I lower my head, not looking at him.

My face stings from where he slapped me, and I don't have to look to know that it's already bruised. My shoulder is dislocated from where it hit the wall. I reach a hand up, popping it back into place, clamping my teeth on my bottom lip to keep from crying out.

As a shifter, I heal fast. It's a good thing I do because this isn't the first time I've dislocated a joint, or even broken a bone because of my father's abuse.

He only abuses me because I'm so small. I'm too weak to defend myself, and I deserve it.

I know that I *don't* deserve a spot at Shifter Academy.

Still, part of me is thrilled at the chance to go. Maybe I can show my pride that I'm not such a runt after all. Maybe if I learn how to fight, my pride will stop seeing me as a burden and start seeing me as part of the family.

Once the pain has subsided, I push myself up off the floor and stand.

It's time to pack a bag.

I'm going to Shifter Academy.

# Friday, August 21
# Fifteen hours.

I have some money hidden inside an old shoe in my closet. It's not a lot, just anything I've managed to scrounge up over the years. I used to do odd jobs for an elderly lady in the pride. I didn't do it for money, but she'd give me a couple of dollars here and there, and over time, that money added up. I never told my dad about the cash. He would want to use the money for booze if I had told him, so I kept it hidden.

I don't know why I saved the money. The alpha always takes care of the members of the pride. Alpha owns a big chunk of land, and each family is provided with a house on that land. They're not the best houses, but it's home. It's enough. All the clothes that I have are hand-me-downs from others in the pride.

Since I am so small, a lot of the clothes are handed down from children in the pride, but I don't mind. Their clothes are cute anyway. Usually they're bright colored, sometimes with fun cartoon characters on them.

Today, I'm glad for that money that I have stored away because that money, less than four hundred dollars, is how I'm going to travel.

You have to take a boat to get to Shifter Academy, but I'm not worried about that. Shifter Academy picks up all their students and brings them to the school. I just have to get from here to the boat.

The boat picks students up in Key West, Florida, which is about six hours south of my small Floridian town. I have no idea how I'm going to get there, but I'm hoping the money will help.

The pride typically drives all the students in large passenger vans. We have about six of them, and they left earlier this morning. When I went to get on, nobody would let me. They said they couldn't handle being in the same vehicle as me for six hours. So now I have to figure out how to get there on my own.

I don't have a smartphone or else I would get an Uber. I've never used an Uber before, but I know older members of the pack use them sometimes when they go out drinking. I have no idea if they could drive me six hours, or even how much it would cost, but it's the only idea I have.

I stand on the side of the road, my suitcase on wheels behind me, and I walk south.

Maybe... maybe I could take a bus. If I'm not mistaken, there is a bus stop about five miles of here. I look at the map in my backpack, just to verify the location, and take off walking.

It's a hot August day in Florida. I pass a local bank, and the sign declares that it's 95 degrees. I imagine the *feels like* temperature is a lot warmer, though. I'm pretty resilient to the heat, but even I am sweating today.

I wish my pride would have just let me on the van with them. I'm sure they're already halfway to Key West this morning, and I'm here, not even out of my town yet. This sucks.

I try to stay positive, but with thoughts of still having to walk another four miles in this heat, it's hard. The only thing that keeps me from turning around and walking back home is the fact that if I did, my pride would be in trouble. That's the last thing I want. And, as much as I would never admit it aloud, I am so excited about going to Shifter Academy. I'm excited about being around other shifters.

I've heard horror stories about the school. Most of them because the other panthers can't stay out of trouble. They get into fights with other shifter types and start trouble in class. I wonder if the other shifters will automatically not like me because I am a panther, or if they will give me the benefit of the doubt.

I also know that there are fae attending Shifter Academy. I've never seen a fairy before, but I am excited to. I hear they are small, like me, but they aren't weak. They give me hope. Like maybe one day I can be strong too, despite my small frame.

As I am walking, I feel a tingle at the back of my neck, and I smell something strange. I'm not sure what the smell is because it's too faint, but I do know that it's a shifter. It's not a cat, so maybe a bear? Or a wolf? I stop and turn my head, trying to get a better whiff. I'm pretty sure that the smell is a wolf, but I can't be certain. I haven't been around any wolves before. I've just been taught what they smell like from my teachers in the pride.

The wolves don't like panthers, so I yank my backpack higher up on my shoulder and begin wheeling my suitcase a little faster behind me, just to be safe.

I wish it wasn't so hot today, maybe then I could run. But if the wolf wanted to attack me, it would have already. Maybe the wolf simply hasn't noticed me, or maybe it's a nice wolf.

My alpha says there are no nice wolves, but I've always wondered if he was wrong. Certainly not *every* wolf shifter is unkind. I have to believe that there is kindness in other places in the world. If I didn't, I would go mad.

Finally, I arrive at the bus station. I grin at the lady behind the glass window as I step up.

"Hello, I would like one ticket to Key West, please." I offer her my nicest smile.

"What happened to your face?" She studies me as she types something into the computer.

I lower my head, letting my hair curtain my face. "I, uh, had an accident."

She nods, but she doesn't look like she believes me. "Bus leaves in twenty three minutes. That'll be sixty dollars."

My mouth falls open.

Sixty dollars?

That's so cheap.

I was so worried I wouldn't have enough money.

I open my wallet and begin to count out dollar bills to her.

She laughs. "That's a lot of dollars, kid. Are you a stripper or something?"

I furrow my brows. "No. I'm a student."

The thought of making it to Shifter Academy makes me smile once more. All of this will be worth it once I get on that boat. My dad hitting me, alpha being mad at me, walking in the heat... it doesn't matter, because my dream is coming true.

I'm attending Shifter Academy.

Once I pass my money over, the lady slides me my ticket. "Good luck in Key West, kid."

"Thanks." I roll my suitcase over and sit in one of the chairs. The air conditioner in here feels nice. My clothes are pretty well soaked through with sweat, but there isn't anything I can do about it now. Once I get to the school, I will shower and get cleaned up.

For now, I will just try and get cooled off.

A few more hours and I'll be there.

I glance at my ticket to see the hours, and I realize just how very wrong I was. Even though it's only a six hour drive to Key West, taking the bus is longer. Much longer. The ticket proclaims it'll take fifteen hours to get there.

Great.

Just freaking great.

# A real friend.

It's after midnight when my bus makes the final stop in Key West. By now, I'm the only one still on the bus. Most others got off at stops along the way.

The bus ride wasn't so bad. I mean, there was this one guy sitting close to me who kept snoring, and there was one lady whose baby screamed all the way to Miami, but she looked like she was having a hard time. I felt kind of bad for her.

I grab my luggage and put my backpack on my shoulders, making my way off the bus. My heart is racing and my palms are sweaty. I'm equally nervous and excited for Shifter Academy. I'm just ready to get there and get settled.

Since it is so late, it's dark outside. I can see in the dark, so that isn't a problem, but I've always been a little scared of the night. I know it's silly. I can shift into a panther. Most people would call me a dangerous predator. But aside from being a panther, I'm also just an eighteen-year-old girl.

When I was younger, I think I was fourteen at the time, I went out for a walk at night, and one of the older boys in my

16

pride thought it would be funny to run me over with his car. It was complete agony while I lay on the ground waiting for my body to heal itself. It took all night for me to be able to even get up and walk home, and then another day to fully heal. I think that was what really made me scared of walking in the dark.

I stay on the sidewalk. Every time a car comes by I step over as far as I can, tensing up. I know that nobody is going to intentionally hit me with their car. The boy in my pride, Cain, is completely messed up in the head. But I'll never admit that out loud. Cain is Alpha George's favorite pack member.

The sound of a car coming my way reaches my ears. This one is driving a little slower than the others, so I turn around and watch as a bright blue Jeep pulls up beside me, stopping in the road. Most girls might be scared by this, but I know if somebody is going to mess with me, I can scare them away. I may be a weak panther, but I'm stronger than any human.

But when the person in the Jeep climbs out, that's when I panic. Because the person in the Jeep definitely isn't a human. It's a wolf shifter. The same wolf shifter that I smelled in my hometown many hours ago.

"Get in." He opens the passenger side door for me.

I shake my head. "I-I-I'm good. Thanks."

I lower my head and start walking again, but the boy comes over and stands in my path.

It's then that I realize just how much of a runt I really am. The top of my head barely reaches this guy's chest. He's got to be at least a foot taller than me, which isn't hard considering I'm only 5'3". I'm the runt of the pride in *every* sense of the word.

"I've watched you walk five miles in the heat, and I only stayed away because I could tell you were scared of me. Then I followed this bus for the past fifteen hours. There is no way in hell that I am going to watch you walk another mile and a half tonight." His brown eyes shift to yellow, and I know he's serious.

He's mad.

"I-I had t-to come..." I lower my head, using my hair to curtain my face.

Why can't I seem to get out any words right now?

As hard as I try not to let this boy see my fear, I know I'm not doing a good job.

I'm useless.

I really am going to embarrass my pride at Shifter Academy.

"Why didn't you come with the rest of your pride?" The boy's voice is softer now, so I look up. His eyes are once again brown. They're so warm. I find myself wanting to reach out and touch him, but I push that thought away. That *would* be silly.

"They didn't want me to ride with them." I shrug my shoulders, trying to show him it's not a big deal. "I'm the runt, so they are embarrassed to be seen with me."

His eyes flash yellow again.

I take a step back. "It's okay. H-h-honest. I know that I'm small. It's why I haven't been allowed at Shifter Academy. Everybody will think the panthers are weak, like me."

His jaw tightens. "Is that what you think?"

I nod. "My alpha told me so."

He takes a deep breath, closing his eyes. When he opens them, they're brown again. "What's your name?"

"Layla Rosewood." I stand up straighter. "I'm a panther shifter."

"I'm Tucker Lewis." He tilts his head. "Layla, will you please get in my Jeep and allow me to give you a ride to the boat?"

I consider his question.

Maybe I should say no. I don't know him at all, and Alpha has always taught us how dangerous wolf shifters are. But Tucker seems nice, and I *am* very tired. I really don't feel like walking a mile and a half right now.

I nod my head. "Yes. That would be lovely. Thank you."

He grins, his brown eyes sparking.

He's happy. He *actually* wants me to ride with him.

It's so weird to be around somebody who isn't disgusted by me, and I'm not sure what to think about it.

Tucker opens the passenger side door of his Jeep for me, and I climb inside. It's tall, so it's a little hard to get in, but I manage to pull myself in. A quick look around the Jeep brings a smile to my face. It seems so... clean. And new.

The door shuts, so I reach over for my seatbelt, buckling in.

Tucker hops into the driver's side. He pauses, looking at me in the passenger seat. His mouth lifts on one side, and I get the feeling that he's really glad I'm riding with him for some reason. Which I don't understand. My pride didn't even want me riding with them. Why does this wolf shifter want me to?

Neither of us say a word as we take off down the street. There isn't a lot of cars out at this time of night, but I notice a couple of girls stumbling down the road, probably after a night of drinking. They appear carefree, like they're having the time of their life. I wonder if my dad ever felt that way when he started drinking.

I want to say alcohol makes my father cruel, but that's not true. My father is simply a cruel man, drunk or not. He has been ever since I can remember. But he's my dad, the only parent I've got.

"I don't recognize you from school." Tucker glances from the road to me.

I push a piece of hair behind my ear. "My alpha wouldn't let me come. I would make the pride look bad."

His knuckles turn white on the steering wheel. "You said that before. Why did your alpha change his mind and allow you to come?"

"I, um, got this letter. It said it's mandatory for me to come. It said if I didn't come, my pride and my alpha would get in a lot of trouble. So my alpha told me to come." I grin, thinking about the school. I can't wait to get there.

"Why was there a bruise on your face this morning?" Tucker is looking at the road when he asks me the question, and I'm glad. It almost seems like he can see right through me, and it's a little intimidating.

I clear my throat. "It was an accident."

His eyes flash to mine. "I'm a wolf shifter."

"I know."

"I can smell a lie."

Oh.

I didn't know that.

That leaves me with two options. I can either tell this wolf the truth, or I can just refuse to answer. Part of me wants to tell him the truth of what happened to me, but I've never spoken a word of it to anybody before. I'm scared of what his reaction will be.

I keep my mouth shut.

"Did somebody hit you?" He pushes further.

Why does he want an answer so bad?

"That's it, isn't it?" He nods his head. "Was it your alpha? Does he hit you?"

I don't want Tucker to think bad about my alpha. We're not allowed to talk ill of him, so I shake my head. "It wasn't Alpha George this time. Alpha only hits me when he absolutely needs to discipline me."

The Jeep comes to an abrupt stop. I figure we are at the boat, but when I look up I see that we're stopped on the side of the street.

21

"Your alpha hits you as discipline?" His mouth is open wide, and I can see the horror in his eyes.

"Yeah. Doesn't your alpha?"

He shakes his head. "Never."

I raise an eyebrow. "Then how do you know that you've done something wrong?"

His mouth opens, then closes again. "I can't even begin to explain how fucked up your alpha is. But when I do something wrong, my alpha sits me down and talks to me about it. He kindly explains what I've done wrong, and he gives me a chance to apologize. He's never hit me, not even when I've probably deserved it."

His alpha sounds... kind.

I feel guilty for the thought.

"Alpha George isn't so bad," I insist. "Please, don't tell anybody what I've told you."

If my alpha found out that I told Tucker about his punishments, there is no telling what he would do to me. Just the thought alone makes me tremble in fear.

"Your secrets are safe with me, Layla. Always." He makes eye contact with me as he says it, and I can feel the truth in his words.

I like the way he says my name.

"Thank you, Tucker." I also like the way his name feels on my lips. It feels right. "Does this mean that we're friends?"

"Yeah. It does." He begins driving his Jeep again.

I am completely giddy. I bounce on my seat a little, angling my body toward him. "I've never had a friend before."

"Then I am honored to be your first."

I smile, thinking Tucker is going to be a good first friend.

It may be a little unconventional for a panther to be friends with a wolf, but I don't care.

I have a friend.

A real friend.

# Beautiful creature.

Whenever Tucker stops the car again, this time we are at the port. He parks his Jeep in a parking lot across the street, but I can't take my eyes off of where the boats are.

I've dreamed of this my whole life, thinking it was just a fantasy, but it's reality now.

I'm really going to Shifter Academy.

"You look really excited about going to school." Tucker taps his fingers on the steering wheel, eyes focused on the boats. He's wearing a frown on his face, like he's dreading going to school.

I want Tucker to like me, and I don't want him to think I'm a nerd, but I am excited. I'm so, so excited.

"I've never been to a school before," I admit. "And nobody in my pride really likes me. I know it's stupid, but

I'm hoping I can make friends here. Maybe I'll even learn some things so I won't be a burden to my pride anymore."

He rubs the scruff on his chin studying me. "I don't know if I should tell you this, but you should be prepared. I just don't want to hurt your feelings."

I offer him a smile. "Don't worry. I don't get my feelings hurt easily. And if you're going to call me a runt, I already know."

"I wasn't going to call you small." He sighs. "At Shifter Academy, panthers aren't very liked. Your pride walks around like they're better than everybody else. I know people will like you once they get to know you, but they might not like you very much at first."

I wasn't expecting that, but I suppose I can see where he is coming from.

My pride can be arrogant. I hate even thinking that about them, but it's true. They think they are better than everybody else. Our alpha reminds us that we are better, but I've never felt the same way. The others... they can't be as bad as Alpha says, right? I mean, Tucker is pretty nice, and he's a wolf.

Tucker gets out of the Jeep first. I push open my door and jump down, turning to grab my suitcase and backpack from the backseat, but I have to stand on the tips of my toes to reach in. Just as I'm about to grab hold, a hand reaches over me and grabs it.

"Thanks." I move as if to grab my backpack from him, but he slings it over one shoulder. A protest rises to my lips,

24

but he starts walking ahead, dragging both of our suitcases behind him, and I stay silent.

I have to run to catch up.

"I can carry my stuff," I insist.

"I've got it." He doesn't stop walking, and he doesn't even turn to acknowledge me.

"I know that I'm small, but I'm not weak." I cross my arms over my chest, wishing everybody would stop seeing me as weak.

He stops in his tracks and turns toward me. "I'm not carrying your stuff because I think you're weak. Just getting to Key West like you did proved that you're not weak, Layla. You're strong. Stronger than any panther I've ever met. I'm carrying your stuff because I'm trying to be a gentleman."

A gentleman.

Huh.

"Nobody has ever showed me such kindness before," I admit. "I'm afraid I might not ever get to repay you."

He shakes his head. "Layla, you don't owe me anything. I promise."

I don't say anything, but I disagree.

I owe him a lot.

Tucker saved me from walking a mile and a half in the dark all alone. He's carrying my luggage for me when I'm exhausted. He has shown me that I don't need to be scared of other shifters like I thought I would. But even more than all that, he has offered to be my friend, which means so much to me.

Someday, I will pay him back.

I follow him down the port and onto the gangway. I'm honestly surprised that the boat is even here for us. I assumed I'd have to wait until morning for them to come pick me up.

Absolute awe keeps me quiet as we walk on board. I follow Tucker to the back of the ship, past the rows of seats. I'm surprised that about half of them are full. He puts our suitcases on the floor beside a seat and motions me to sit on the side, positioning me closest to the edge of the ship.

I'm excited as I take my seat. I can look over the edge and see water. Even though I just sat down, I stand, looking over the edge to get a better view.

"Tucker, you're the one who held up the boat? Why am I not surprised?"

As I turn to face the boy who addressed Tucker, I scent that he is a tiger. I completely tense up, scared that he is going to attack me.

My alpha *hates* tiger shifters more than any other species. I am hoping that the hate doesn't go both ways, because this tiger is huge. I couldn't defend myself against him.

The boy isn't quite as big as Tucker, but he's still scary as hell.

"And who is this beautiful creature?" The boy looks at me.

I lower my head, trying to make myself appear as small as possible. None of my pride is here to help me if this guy decides to attack me.

"Levi, you're scaring her." Tucker growls the words out at the tiger, but gently touches my back. "Hey, it's all right. Levi isn't going to hurt you."

I take a deep breath and raise my head.

Levi isn't staring at me like he wants to attack. In fact, he's smiling.

He holds out his hand. "I am so very sorry I scared you. I'm Levi Young."

I look at his hand. "I'm Layla Rosewood."

Does he want to shake hands with me?

His hand falls, and he looks at me with his brows furrowed. "So you're new?"

I am not used to so many people talking to me. This is weird.

Does Levi want to be my friend too?

"Levi, you should take your seat. I think we're about to leave," Tucker says, rescuing me from having to respond to the guy.

I don't mean to be rude. I'm sure Levi is nice. I'm just honestly a little frightened of him.

Levi nods, grinning at me. "Nice to meet you, Layla. I look forward to getting to know you better at school."

I just stare at him, my mouth hanging open.

I think he actually means that.

The boat rumbles a bit, and I feel it start to move as Levi walks back to his seat. He glances over at me one last time and winks before sitting down.

I turn my attention to Tucker, who is studying me.

"Levi is... very friendly." I chew on the side of my lip, trying to form a coherent thought, but I am so overwhelmed.

"Yeah, he is." Tucker's jaw tightens, and I wonder if Tucker likes Levi. He almost seems... annoyed with him. "You should get some sleep. It's a good ride to the school."

I swallow hard, nodding. "Yeah, okay."

I am pretty tired.

But I don't know if I can sleep sitting on this bench. I don't even have anywhere to rest my head.

Before I can think too hard about it, Tucker pulls me toward him. He only touches me where my shirt is, and he lays my head on his chest.

"This won't be comfortable for you," I mumble, but my eyes are already getting heavy.

Tucker is comfortable.

"Sleep," he commands.

And I find myself drifting off before I can fight it.

With my head on the chest of a wolf, I feel safer than I have in a long time.

## Saturday, August 22
# But how?

When I open my eyes again, I am met with the bright morning sun. I snuggle back down into a very comfortable pillow as I let my mind begin to awaken.

*Oh.*

My eyes widen and heat flushes my cheeks when I realize that my comfortable pillow is Tucker's chest. I can't believe I slept on him all night, but I have to admit that I have never slept so well before.

I hope I didn't snore.

I sit up, surprised to see him watching me. But then again, I did just spend an entire night snuggled up to his chest.

"Sorry." I frown, hoping I haven't completely offended my new friend. "You should have woken me."

"I liked you lying on me." He shrugs, like it's not a big deal.

Maybe it's not. Maybe this is just how friends are.

Reluctantly, I smile at him. "Thank you."

"We are almost to the school."

My eyes widen and I look from him to the side of the boat. There is water as far as the eye can see, and it doesn't seem like we are anywhere near the school at all. But just as I think that, it's like a veil is pulled from my eyes and I see that we're coming upon an island.

Whoa.

It's magic. That is the only word I can use to describe it.

A castle sits on an island off in the distance and my heart races with anticipation, excitement, and dread.

This is everything I've dreamed of and more.

But what if life here is miserable? I know my pride doesn't want me here.

"What has caused the pained look on your face?" Tucker asks, distracting me from my thoughts.

I sigh, turning toward him. "I'm just worried. I know that nobody in my pride wants me here. What if... what if they try to make things miserable for me?"

There really is no 'what if.' I know them, and I know they *will* make things hard for me.

"I won't let them." Tucker nods, like the decision is already final.

"How can you do anything about it though?" I question. "Won't I be rooming with my pride? Isn't that how it works? They separate us by what kind of shifter we are."

He looks at me, his lips turning up in the corner. "Normally, yes. But you are different."

My mouth falls open. "How?"

He reaches his hand up ever so gently, and he traces his thumb on the side of my cheek. "Because you are my mate."

I want to deny his words, but I can't.

My heart races and my stomach fills with butterflies from his touch. And there is no doubt in my mind at all that Tucker Lewis is mine.

"How?" I whisper. "You're a wolf, and I'm a panther." I have never heard of any panther having a mate of a different species. It's not... normal.

"I don't know, but it's true." He tucks a piece of hair behind my ear, and I find myself leaning into his touch.

My heart feels so full that it could burst.

But just as quickly, I panic.

My pride is going to disown me.

My alpha told me not to do anything to embarrass him, and this is going to do just that. He's going to kick me out of the pride.

"What's wrong, Layla?" Tucker asks, his thumb still drawing circles on my cheek.

"My alpha..." I shake my head. "He will never accept this. He will kick me out of the pride."

"My alpha will accept you as a member of my pack. Don't worry. You will still have family." He says it so easily, but it can't be that easy, can it?

I have so many questions, but we arrive at the academy, and all other thoughts vanish.

The castle is bigger than I imagined it to be. I've seen pictures of the school before, but when I imagined it, it was never this big. I should've known the school would have to be huge to accommodate all the students.

We line up to get off the boat, and I see the boy I met last night, Levi, standing in front of us. I feel a little more at ease around him now. If he were going to attack me, I think he would have done so by now. I also don't think Tucker would allow anybody to attack me. At least, I hope not.

A big part of me wants to deny that Tucker is my mate, but when I try, my mind completely rejects it. There is no way to fake the feeling that I get whenever we touched. He *is* my mate. It just doesn't make sense. He's a wolf, and I'm a panther.

"Don't think so hard." Tucker grabs my hand and squeezes it.

It's so comforting to be touched like this. I can't remember the last time somebody touched me that hasn't made me flinch from fear. Whenever my dad touches me, it's always in anger. It's to slap me, or punch me, or push me. He's never touched me to comfort me. He's never even looked at me with anything other than disdain.

Levi glances back at me, so I offer him a smile. My stomach clinches when I think about how rude I was to him last night. I hope he can understand, given the circumstances.

Now that we are standing, I can see that Levi is slightly shorter than Tucker, but only by a couple of inches. His brown hair sticks up all over, probably because we just slept on a boat. I'm sure my hair doesn't look any better.

My hair is strawberry blonde, and it is naturally wavy. I'm sure it's frizzy from the walk I did yesterday, along with the long bus ride.

Levi grins back, his blue eyes sparkling in the sunlight. "Good morning, Layla."

"Morning, Levi."

He glances down at mine and Tucker's intertwined hands. He raises an eyebrow at Tucker, but he doesn't say anything.

He probably wonders why Tucker is holding my hand. There is no way that he thinks I'm Tucker's mate, no way at all. Because wolves and panthers are *never* mates.

Come to think of it, how did Tucker know that I am his mate? He seemed to know before he even touched me.

"What are you thinking about?" Tucker turns to me.

"How do you know I'm thinking about something?"

He grins. "Because you are easy to read, little one."

Ah.

I suppose that is true. I've never been able to hide my emotions, which has only made the pride pick on me more.

"How did you know?" I ask, wording the question carefully since Levi is listening in. I don't want Levi to know that Tucker is my mate unless Tucker wants to tell him. Isn't he embarrassed of me? I don't want to make things worse.

"Know what?" Tucker cocks his head.

I clear my throat, trying to come up with the right words. "Um... well... you said you followed me from my hometown. And you gave me a ride here from the bus station. Because you *knew*..."

He nods, as he realizes what I'm asking. "You want to know how I knew you are my mate before we touched?"

I nod, my cheeks growing warm.

I notice Levi's face has turned ashen white, and his mouth has dropped open in complete shock.

I knew it wasn't normal. He's probably questioning if our bond is even real.

"Wolves can smell their mates. No touch is required," he informs me.

I didn't know that.

That's kind of cool, actually.

"Bears can smell their mates too." Levi seems to recover from his shock.

"Then why can't I smell it too?" I wonder.

"Because cat shifters can't smell as well as wolves." Tucker shrugs. "I guess it's just how it is."

"But we're faster." Levi wiggles his eyebrows. "And more agile."

Yes, I suppose he is right. Wolves are superior is some ways, and cats are superior in others.

"But this isn't normal." I motion between Tucker and myself. "Panthers don't mate with shifters who aren't of the same species."

"Yeah they do," Tucker counters.

Levi nods, backing up Tucker's claim.

I ponder that. "Then why have I never heard of it happening?"

"Maybe your alpha kept it from you," Tucker suggests. "It's rare, but it happens."

Before I can form a rebuttal to defend Alpha George, the line to get off the boat starts moving, and I take my first step onto Shifter Academy grounds.

I'm really here.

I'm really a Shifter Academy student.

I'm so happy, I could cry.

# Something to cry about.

A cobblestone pathway leads to the castle. Palm trees are lined up along the sides, and I see a big mango tree off in the distance. I wonder if we're allowed to pick mangos off to eat, because that would be awesome.

There is a very large double door that leads inside the school. It's a glass door, with a gold frame. As I walk through the doorway, I realize the entryway must be over ten feet tall.

Once we make our way inside, I feel smaller than ever. When I look up, the ceiling just keeps going, at least five stories high, and a large chandelier hangs from the top.

The floors are white marble, with a gold pattern. I've never seen anything like this before. It's incredible.

Tucker tugs on my hand, pulling me away from the group that is now headed up the stairs.

"Come on," he says.

"Where are we going?" I question, but still follow him.

"To talk to Margot Westwood about your room."

I suppose that makes sense. Since I am new, I don't have a room assigned to me yet. I wonder momentarily who they will place with me. Possibly with another panther. I cringe, thinking whoever gets stuck with me is going to hate it.

We enter a room that has a spiral staircase leading upward. There is somebody sitting at a desk at the bottom of the stairs, but it's not Margot Westwood. It's a younger girl, a wolf shifter. She grins when she sees Tucker.

"Tucker." She stands from the desk, her eyes lighting up. She has yet to notice or acknowledge me.

"Oh, hey." Tucker turns his head toward the girl, his eyes narrowed like he's concentrating.

The girl's face falls. "Melanie."

Oh.

Oh!

He forgot her name. That's quite awkward, considering the big crush she has on him.

"Melanie, right. We're just going up to see Margot." Tucker lifts up the hand that is holding mine.

Her eyes narrow in on the hand, and she looks up, confusion on her face. "She's a... panther."

"Yep." Tucker pulls on my hand and we walk away from Melanie, who still appears confused. And I get it. What is a wolf doing hanging out with a panther?

We walk up the metal staircase that seems to go on forever. Tucker never loosens his grip on my hand, and I'm glad that he's here with me. I'm not sure what I would do if I were here alone. I'd be walking around aimlessly, not knowing where to go. I could try to ask a member of my pride to help me, but they would most likely just ignore me like they do at home.

The other panthers spend most of their time either ignoring me, or being cruel to me. I've grown to accept it. It's not so bad, anyway. I have learned to be independent and not rely on anybody. I know that goes against everything the pride stands for, because we are supposed to depend on one another, but they never give me a choice.

I want to belong. It's my deepest desire that I've never told anybody before. I want friends, and a family. I want my pride to accept me like I have accepted myself.

Being little isn't so bad. I can get into places that bigger panthers can't. And I am really sneaky and fast. But nobody sees that. They just can't get over the fact that I'm not strong. All they seem to care about is strength.

We reach the top of the staircase and walk into a large, oval office. I've seen pictures of this room during my studies, but experiencing it in person is so different.

The floors in here are the same marble with gold patterns, like downstairs. There is a large red rug in the middle of the space, and a massive L-shaped desk. A woman sits at the desk, doing something on her laptop. When she notices we are standing in her office, she pauses her work to address us.

"Can I help you, Tucker?" the woman—Margot Westwood, I think—asks.

Of course Margot Westwood knows Tucker. I mean, she's a wolf too. Doesn't that mean they're from the same pack? Plus, she's the dean of the school, and he's a senior. She's likely seen him around the school.

"I'd like you to meet Layla Rosewood." Tucker pulls me up next to him, putting his arm around me.

Margot's eyes light up. "Layla, it's so nice to have you here. I've been trying to get you to this school for years."

My eyes widen. "Really?"

"But your alpha..." She rolls her eyes. "I went around him and didn't give him a choice. He seemed really upset about sending you here."

I nod, lowering my head. "Because I make my pride look bad."

Tucker *growls* at my words. "I'd like to meet this alpha."

"Me too," Margot agrees.

I peek up and see that both Tucker's and Margot's eyes are glowing yellow, meaning their wolves are close to the surface. But just as quickly as their eyes turned yellow, they go back to their normal color.

I'm confused by their actions, but I don't question it. I just observe them, trying to understand wolves a little better. So far, they're just confusing.

Margot focuses her gaze on Tucker. "I'm curious why you took an interest in Layla. I always thought you were more of a lone wolf."

Tucker stands up straighter, a smile on his face. "Layla is my mate."

Margot's eyes widen. "Wow. Congratulations." She looks at me. "Both of you. It's incredible to meet your mate so young."

"Thank you." I cast my gaze downward.

People in my pride don't like it if I make prolonged eye contact with them. I think they worry the rest of the pride will shun them for talking to me. I can't blame them for thinking that, because it's probably true.

"Who are you going to room me with?" My voice is shaky, even to my own ears. "My pride... t-th-they don't like me. If I'm with one of them, they'll be miserable to even be in my presence. So maybe you could put me with a different species. I promise I won't be a bother. I just... I want to do well, and I don't want anybody to be annoyed with me."

Margot huffs. "Layla, don't worry about your pride. You are getting your own room."

I lift my head to stare at her, sucking in a breath. "My own room?"

She nods.

That sounds incredible. I would never be in anybody's way, and I won't be a burden to anybody in my pride.

"Whenever a shifter finds their mate, we always give the newly mated couple their own living space," Margot informs me.

Realization hits me.

I actually won't be living alone. Because Tucker is my mate. And thinking about that brings on all new thoughts. Like... the fact that mates have to complete a mate bond.

My face grows warm as I think about what completing the mate bond entails.

I've never done anything physical with a guy. Never a kiss. Not even a hug. Tucker is the first guy to ever touch me in an intimate way. How am I supposed to jump from never touching to... sex?

"Tucker will stay in his old room until you're ready to be intimate, of course," Margot insists.

Tucker nods. "Absolutely. Layla, I would never rush you into anything you're not comfortable with."

He is a nicer mate than I deserve. I know I shouldn't make him wait to complete the mate bond, but I'm scared of doing *that*. Just thinking about it makes me sick to my stomach with worry.

I tuck a piece of hair behind my ear. "That doesn't seem fair to Tucker."

Margot stands up from her desk and makes her way around to our side. "We find that younger mates take longer to complete their mate bond. It's nothing to be ashamed of.

You're young, and completing the mate bond, merging your souls together forever, shouldn't be taken lightly."

Merging my soul with Tucker's sounds really nice.

"That's not what I'm scared of." I look down, my face growing warm. "I've never even *kissed* a boy. What if I'm really bad at the actual mating part?"

Margot clears her throat. "Ah, right. Well... Tucker, I'm going to let you help Layla to her room."

Tucker grabs onto my hand again. "Come on, Layla."

I can hear the smile in Tucker's voice, so I look up and see that he has a huge smile on his face. I worried that he wouldn't want to be mates with me when he realized how inexperienced I am. It's a relief to know that's not the case.

We exit Margot's office but stop at the top of the stairs. I'm confused until I feel Tucker's arms go around me. He squeezes me against him.

I don't know that I've ever been hugged in my life. But this... this is nice. Really nice. I wrap my arms around him, squeezing him back.

I don't know how long Tucker holds me, but eventually he pulls back. When he does, he wipes under my eyes. It's then that I realize I'd been crying. I didn't mean to. I *never* cry. It's just, being held like that, it was everything I've ever wanted and more.

"I needed that, and I hope it was okay." He ever so gently wipes the tears away.

I nod. "I liked that. A lot. It was my first hug."

Tucker's entire body stiffens and his eyes get shiny, like he's about to cry too. But then he blinks and he smiles. I can tell that the smile is forced now, but I don't understand why. He is a complicated man, and I can't even begin to understand his mind.

"Want me to show you to your room?" He grabs onto my hand again.

"Yes." I grin widely at the thought of seeing my new home for the next nine months.

I'm really at Shifter Academy. There is no going back.

For the first time in I don't remember how long, I am happy. Truly and genuinely happy.

I just hope whatever happiness I have lasts.

If my pride sees me smiling... They'll give me something to cry about. That's just the way it is for a runt like me.

# New home.

When we get to the door that leads to my room, my hands are shaking with anticipation, and I feel so happy that I could cry.

I get my own room.

I don't have to share.

I don't have to be a burden on anybody else.

I remind myself that this room is supposed to be for Tucker and me. At some point he'll be in here too, but I try not to think about that just yet.

Tucker opens the door, motioning for me to walk in first. I hesitantly take a step forward. I notice, as the door opens farther, it doesn't squeak. At my house, I always had to open my door very carefully so I wouldn't wake my dad, because it squeaked so loudly. Here, I don't have to worry about that.

I know it's silly to be so excited about having a door that doesn't make a noise, but I love that I don't have to worry about disrupting anybody. I can come and go as I please.

The floor in my room is the same marble that I've seen everywhere else in the castle. I've grown to love the floors, but I bet cleaning them is a nightmare.

In the middle of my room, there is a huge bed, reminding me once again that this room was never meant for just one person. The bed appears to be a king sized, but it may be even bigger than that. It's so long. I glance at Tucker who stands a foot taller than me. He definitely needs a bed this big.

The comforter is white and fluffy. At home, I've been using the same pink comforter for as long as I can remember. Most of the stuffing has come out of it, and I get cold a lot at night. Here, there's no way I will be cold. If anything, I'll be hot under all that fluff.

There is also a huge white rug that takes up a lot of space on the floor. I am careful not to walk over it with my shoes, not wanting to dirty it up. But I'm excited to feel the rug with my bare feet. I wonder if it's as soft as it looks.

A couch sits in the corner of the room, and a TV hangs on the wall. I've never had a TV before. My dad had one in the living room, and sometimes I would catch something he was watching, but one night when he was drunk he knocked it down and broke it. It never got replaced after that.

My sweeping study of the room comes to a halt when I notice a desk, and I can't fight the grin it brings to my face.

Any homework I had when I was homeschooled always had to be completed at the dining room table. I've never had a desk before, and this one I'm grateful to have to myself.

As we continue to look around the room, I feel like my heart is going to burst with happiness. This is *my* room. It's my home. And it's safe from everybody.

Tucker shows me the walk-in closet next. My suitcase and backpack are sitting in there. I will have to unpack, but my stuff won't even fill a tenth of this space.

After the closet we head into the bathroom, and my breath catches in my throat.

The bathroom is bigger than my old bedroom. Heck, it might even be bigger than the whole house.

There is a private door with a toilet behind it, which is kind of cool. There is a double sink, once again reminding me that this is meant for Tucker and me to share. The bathtub is huge—big enough for at least two people—and I can't wait to soak in there.

The shower is the best, though. It's one of those showers that rains water down from the ceiling. And the entire thing is actually bigger than my old room. Five people could probably fit in it, all at the same time. Even if the people are as big as Tucker.

What am I going to do with all this space?

"You've been quiet," Tucker comments, as we walk back into the main room.

I nod. "I think I'm in shock."

Like, complete and utter shock.

"I don't deserve things this nice," I admit. I drop my gaze to the ground, not wanting to see the expression on his face when he agrees with me.

Tucker puts his hand under my chin, nudging me gently so that I look at him. "You deserve the world, Layla."

My heart swells at his words.

Why does Tucker think so highly of me? Doesn't he see how small and insignificant I am? Doesn't he see that I'm weak? Doesn't he know that even my own pride doesn't want me? Not even my *dad*. Yet, he looks at me like I am a prize, and I don't quite know how to handle it.

"I-I want to clean up." I turn away from him, unable to handle the intenseness of his gaze.

"Okay." He takes a step back, putting some distance between us. "Do you mind if I wait here while you clean up?"

I glance over at him, wondering *why* he wants to stay here. I imagined he would want to get away from me as quickly as he could.

"I would like that," I admit. Because I'm not ready to say goodbye to Tucker just yet. I want him here. Always.

He smiles, and then strides out of the bathroom and over to my bed, where he promptly takes a seat. I don't take a breath until I shut the door behind him, my hand against my racing heart, wondering how I can already feel so much for a boy I just met. But I suppose he *is* my mate. And this is normal for mates.

But even as I have that thought, I wonder if it's true. Does everybody feel this strongly about their mates? Because I have seen other panther mates, and they seem to despise one another.

I hope Tucker and I never hate each other, but I realize I don't have anything to worry about.

Tucker isn't going to hate me.

Not ever.

## Beautifully small.

I take the longest shower I've ever taken in my life.

After walking five miles and being on a bus for fifteen hours, I was pretty gross. And since I was wearing flip flops, the bottoms of my feet were actually black.

Shampoo, conditioner, soap, and face wash were already in the shower, which is a relief. My own supply of soap was getting low, and I ran out of conditioner about a week ago.

The panther in charge of handing out supplies refused to give me any conditioner. I was worried that they wouldn't even give me soap when the time came, so I'm glad I'm here.

The shampoo and conditioner here is a much better quality than the ones I had back home. My hair feels so soft as I wash the conditioner out. And the smell... It's wonderful. Like peaches and cream.

Once I'm finished with my shower, I wrap a big, fluffy white towel around me and make my way over to the sink. Under the cabinet, there is an unopened toothbrush and a tube of toothpaste. I grab it and brush my teeth, thankful to finally be getting clean.

I must have looked atrocious. It's a wonder that Tucker even wanted to be seen with me.

Pulling open a drawer, I find a hair brush, along with some leave in conditioner. I grab them out and begin to slowly brush through my tangles. Once that is done, I smile at my reflection, satisfied with how clean I am.

I go to get dressed, when I remember...

I definitely didn't bring clothes into the bathroom with me.

And Tucker is still in my room.

I peer at myself in the mirror.

The towel covers me well enough. The thing goes to my knees, which is longer than any of the dresses I wear. It's modest enough, so I leave the bathroom and step into my room.

Tucker is coming out of the closet as I walk into my room. I wonder what he was doing in there, but all other thoughts disappear when his eyes meet mine.

He slowly scans my body up and down, and he looks at me as if I walked out of the bathroom completely naked.

I glance down to make sure the towel is still there. It is.

"I forgot to bring clothes with me." I grip the top of my towel. It's on tight, but better safe than sorry.

Tucker shuts his mouth, like he just realized that his jaw was hanging open. "I, uh..." He shakes his head. "Your clothes..." He points at the closet, at a complete loss for words.

I tuck a piece of my wet hair behind my ear. "I'm just going to get dressed."

I go to pass him, but he grabs onto my wrist, stopping me.

My skin feels as though it's on fire where his skin touches mine.

"I went into the closet to hang up your clothes for you." He loosens his grip on my wrists as I turn to him. "That isn't everything, right?"

My face grows warm, and I nod.

Those clothes are literally my only possessions that I have in the entire world.

"I know that your pride sucks, but what about your parents? Don't they care?" Tucker's voice sounds off, so I look him in the eyes. The color has completely drained from his face, and his chin is trembling.

"I don't have a mom." I pause, wondering how to word the next part. "And my dad... he is ashamed to have me as a daughter. My clothes are handed down from younger members of my pride. I am about the same size as most of the eleven or twelve year old's."

He lets out a long breath, his face turning from ashen white to red. His eyes flash yellow, then back to brown before he responds.

"There is a member of my pack who is about your size. She's a little bit shorter than you, but her and her mates are here for an alpha council meeting." His voice is surprisingly calm. "I called her, and she is going to bring you some clothes to get by on. I've already called my mom and asked her to ship you some clothes to the school."

I stumble backwards in shock. "What? Why?" I shake my head. "No, Tucker. It's too much. I'm not worth that. I'm just a runt."

He clenches his jaw. "Please stop saying that about yourself."

"But it's true."

"You're not a runt. You're just... small. Beautifully small." He gently touches my cheek with his thumb. "And perfect. Unbelievably perfect."

I close my eyes, wishing I could see what he sees.

When he pulls his hand back, I open my eyes again. "Wait. Did you say you have a pack member who is *shorter* than me?"

He grins, nodding his head. "Yeah."

My mouth falls open. "That's insane."

"She's my future alpha's mate." He stands up straighter, puffing his chest out.

He's happy to tell me about this girl. And I know it's only to make me feel better, but it *does* make me feel better.

Not every shifter is tall. That makes me excited.

I can't wait to meet this wolf shifter. If she's smaller than I am, and she is strong enough to be the alpha's *mate*, then maybe I do have hope. Maybe I can learn to fight. Maybe I can be strong. It's all I've ever wanted—to not be an embarrassment to my pride. I want to be able to fight by their side and prove that I am worthy.

A knock on the door disrupts my thoughts.

"That's her."

Tucker walks to the door and opens it. I'm still standing there in a towel, but as he opens the door, I realize it's too late to do anything about it.

A girl who is shorter than me stands on the other side. She walks past Tucker when she spots me, a huge grin on her face.

"You must be Layla." Her arms are full of clothes as she looks up at me. "Some of my skirts might be a little short on you, but they should be fine. We're about the same size." She cocks her head. "You're awfully skinny."

I nod. "I'm the runt of my pride."

Tucker growls.

Yikes.

I forgot that he doesn't like when I call myself a runt, even if it is what I am.

"You smell different." I slap a hand over my mouth when I realize what I said. "Oh, my God. I am so sorry. That was rude."

She grins. "Don't worry about it. I'm half wolf, half fae. So that's why I smell different."

Tucker walks over, takes the clothes from her hands, and sets them on the bed. "I really appreciate you bringing these clothes for Layla."

"No problem," the short, black haired fairy says.

"What's your name?" I ask her, once I realize she never told me.

"Penelope." She holds out her hand to shake mine. "It's nice to meet you."

I accept her hand shake. "You too."

I'm surprised that Penelope is being so nice to me. I know that when her people were threatened, the panthers decided not to aid them. It didn't surprise me that Alpha George decided not to help, he doesn't like to get involved in anybody else's fights. But I was a little embarrassed that we didn't help them.

Penelope looks between Tucker and me. "I should really get going. Aiden and Liam are waiting in the hallway for me."

"Thank you again," I tell her, as she turns away.

"You're welcome." She heads out of the door, shutting it behind her.

I stare at the closed door.

Penelope was so nice. I didn't expect it. I mean, Tucker has been so nice to me. And that tiger shifter I met on the boat was kind. But I just thought people here would see me as my pride does. I don't quite know how to handle the fact that they're nice to me.

I turn to Tucker.

"You should get dressed." His face is red as he says it.

Right.

I grab a dress from the pile of clothes and step into the closet to get dressed.

The dress that Penelope brought is really pretty. There are no sparkles or unicorns on it. Instead, this dress was made for somebody who is my age. It's white with a pink flower print, and it's actually not tight across my chest for once. It fits perfectly. It's weird to have clothes that actually fit right.

The length isn't too short either. It goes down to about mid thigh, which is not that much shorter than what I normally wear. I like it.

I walk out of the closet, feeling confident about how I look. I actually feel pretty for once in my life, and I'm excited to see what Tucker thinks.

Tucker's mouth is wide open as he stares at me.

"You are gorgeous," he proclaims, taking a step toward me. "Like, wow."

My face grows warm at his compliment. "Thanks."

"Now that you're cleaned up and dressed, do you want to check out the rest of the school?"

I nod. "That sounds great."

Tucker grabs my hand, and the two of us head out the door.

I'm eager to explore the school.

# My own pride.

As we descend the stairs, I see a lot of shifters walking around.

Not just shifters, I realize, but there are fae too. There aren't as many fae as there are shifters, but it's still nice to see them walking around. I feel like I'll fit right in with them, with me being as short as I am.

Tucker holds my hand, and I'm so glad for his encouragement. I'm not sure I'd be as confident to explore the school without him.

I'm kind of nervous. I wonder what these people will think of me. Will they be nice, like Tucker, Levi, and Penelope? Or will they look at me and only see a runt, like the rest of my pride?

A few members of my pride walk around. One of them notices me and rolls her eyes, looking away. They're all pretending like they don't see me, which is just fine with me. I'd much rather they ignore me than for them to pick on me.

I wonder what they will think when they learn that my mate is a wolf.

I suppose it doesn't matter what they think. Tucker says his alpha will accept me into their pack, so even if Alpha George kicks me out, I will still have a shifter family. At least, I hope. Tucker seemed confident. And their alpha accepted

Penelope into their pack, despite the fact that she is part fae. So maybe I do have a chance.

Alpha George would *never* let anybody else in our pride. He seems to be under the impression that panthers are better than everybody else.

As we roam through the academy, Tucker points out where things are located along the way, making sure I know where all my classes are, and where the cafeteria is.

He takes me into the common room, where all the shifters hang out together. It's completely amazing to see. There are tigers talking to bears, and wolves talking to lions, and fae talking to ravens. It's a sight to behold. The only shifters that keep to themselves are the panthers, which makes me feel a little ashamed.

Why won't the panthers talk to any other species?

I know what Shifter Academy is for. It's to unite all the species of shifters, and now fae too. We're supposed to make connections and friends outside of our species. This is supposed to help us not go to war with one another. It's part of the alliance. It warms my heart to see that everybody is taking it so seriously.

Except...

The panthers.

I sigh, thinking I will just have to be nice to everybody. I will show them that all the panthers aren't bad. Really.

The others are just following Alpha George's orders. I know they have to be. He probably told them not to talk to anybody. But me... he never told me anything, except not to embarrass the pride.

Tucker squeezes my hand. "What do you think?"

"This school is amazing," I say, in complete awe. "It's everything I've ever dreamed it would be."

He smiles, seemingly proud that I like the school. "I'm so glad that you're here, Layla. Who knows if I ever would have found you if you hadn't been on the street that day. My wolf smelled you." He pauses, shaking his head. "I usually take another route to school. I take the quick route. But for some reason, yesterday I decided to take the scenic route. I got off on that exit to fill my Jeep up with gas, and that's when I smelled you."

I am glad he took the scenic route too. I'm about to tell him so, when I hear somebody shouting.

"Stay away from her."

I turn toward the voice, wondering who is about to get into a fight. That's when I realize the guy who spoke was talking to Tucker.

What the heck is happening?

My mouth drops open as a very tall guy barrels toward us.

I recognize the guy's scent. It's very earthy, like grass and tree sap. He smells good, but I tense as I realize that he is a bear.

I should've known by his size alone. He stands over Tucker by a good six inches, and his arms are literally bigger around than my waist. He could snap me in half with one hand if he wanted to.

The bear shifter's eyes are narrowed as he looks at Tucker, and I can't tell what color his eyes are because they are black right now. His bear is close to the surface.

I take a step between the guy and Tucker, wanting to protect my mate.

That was probably dumb. If anybody has a chance to actually beat this guy in a fight, it's Tucker, not me. But now that I'm here, I'm not going to back down. I will show Tucker that I am a worthy mate. And maybe I can show the others that size doesn't matter. I can be brave.

The line between bravery and stupidity is very thin right now, and I'm not sure which side of the line I stand on.

Tucker pulls me back so that he is in front of me.

"I said get your hands off her." The bear shifter talks slowly, enunciating each word carefully. He growls as he ends his sentence. I don't know if he growled to make himself more intimidating, but it's working. If he would've growled at me, I probably would've pissed myself.

"Why do you care if I touch her?" Tucker takes a step closer to the bear, poking him in the chest.

Didn't anybody ever tell Tucker not to poke a bear?

Or was it not to poke a sleeping bear?

Either way, poking a bear is *bad*.

"She is mine." The bear swings his gaze away from Tucker, his eyes meeting mine for the first time. The black melts away, revealing chocolate brown eyes.

He's kind of beautiful.

But I know I shouldn't feel that way about somebody other than my mate, so I push those thoughts aside.

Tucker cocks his head. "What do you mean she's yours? She's my mate."

The bear looks from me back to Tucker. "You are mistaken, wolf. She is my mate."

My mouth falls open.

The bear thinks he's my mate too?

"I'm sure you're very nice," I tell the bear. "But Tucker is right. He's my mate."

The bear steps past Tucker, invading my personal space. I'm about to tell him to back off when he reaches over and grabs onto my hand ever so gently.

Feelings rush through me. My heart races and my panther declares this man as mine.

But how can he be mine when Tucker is mine?

"I'm confused." I look between Tucker and the bear who hasn't even told me his name yet.

Tucker steps back a little but still holds my other hand. "Wow. This is... interesting."

The bear nods, looking at me. "What is your name, panther?"

"Layla Rosewood." I'm still so confused about what is going on, but I know there is plenty of time for my questions to be answered. Right now, I just want to get to know this beautiful boy in front of me. I need to know his name.

"Layla." His thumb gently strokes my hand lightly. "I am Mateo Fisher."

"Mateo," I repeat.

He closes his eyes when I say his name, and he takes a deep breath, almost as if he is savoring the way I say his name.

I feel the same way when he says mine.

I look from Mateo to Tucker. "What is going on, Tucker? I'm confused. How can I have two mates?"

Tucker shrugs. "It's not common for a shifter to have more than one mate, but it happens. My future alpha shares his mate with three other wolves."

Penelope.

Right.

She has four mates.

So it's not really that strange that I have two. But my mates aren't even the same species. One is a bear, and one is a wolf. And I am a panther. So where does that leave us?

"We have a lot to talk about." Mateo focuses on Tucker. "Should we go somewhere more private?"

That is when I realize that the entire room is looking at us, including the panthers.

When I make eye contact with a guy from my pack, he wrinkles his nose in disgust, like he can't believe I'm a member of the same pride as him.

To be honest, that is probably *exactly* what he's thinking right now. It's what they're all thinking. But for the first time, I don't care what my pride thinks, because I am happy. I am *so* happy. Standing here, holding hands with Mateo and Tucker, my heart feels fuller than it ever has in my life. And I realize, this is what belonging somewhere feels like.

I don't need the panthers.

Not anymore.

I have my own pride now.

# Runt.

I have two boys in my room.

No. Tucker and Mateo are not *boys*. They are *men*.

I am nervous as I consider what all of this means. Tucker and Mateo are both my mates. But they're strong. I'm sure their alphas are proud of them. They're different from me in every single way possible. Once they get to know me, they will see it too. They will see the girl that the rest of my pride sees. They'll see... weakness. They'll see a runt.

Mateo narrows his gaze on me. "Why do I smell self-loathing?"

My eyes widen.

He can *smell* it?

"She does that a lot," Tucker explains, taking a seat on the edge of my bed.

Tucker can smell it too?

My brain feels like it's going to explode from all that I'm learning about my mates.

"But why?" Mateo steps closer to me, and I feel so intimidated by him.

Wow. He's freaking tall. A whole foot and a half taller than me.

I swallow hard, looking up at him. "I've never met anybody as tall as you before."

He cracks a smile, making him slightly less intimidating. I don't think he's going to hurt me, but it wouldn't be hard for him, if he changed his mind.

"You're really small for a shifter." Mateo cocks his head, studying me.

I lower my head, letting my hair curtain my face. "I am the runt of my pride."

"What the hell? Who told you that?" Mateo stands back, his head whipping back as if I've slapped him in the face.

"My alpha, my pride, and even my dad." I am brave enough to glance up again, but I only look because I'm curious. What is making Mateo react like this toward me? I don't quite understand him yet. "I know that I am small and weak. I'm sorry that you've gotten stuck with a mate like me. If you don't want to be with me, I would understand."

Mateo's eyes flash black, and I notice a vein in his neck popping out.

He's mad.

Really mad.

And even though I am so disappointed, this is the reaction I was expecting from both him and Tucker. I expected them to be angry for getting stuck with a runt like me as their mate.

Isn't it bad enough that Tucker is stuck with me? Now Mateo is too, and I feel so, so bad for the both of them.

He takes a step closer. I want to back away, but I stay to prove that I'm not as weak as he thinks I am. He puts his hand on the side of my face. His touch is so gentle for somebody so big.

"Layla Rosewood, there is nobody in the world I would rather have as my mate than you." His words are so soft, despite the fact that his bear is so close to the surface. Whoever he is mad at, it's not me.

I sigh, leaning into his touch.

I am already used to being touched so intimately. It's strange, but I think I am addicted.

I'm in complete awe at Mateo's words. He *wants* to be my mate. And that makes me happy, because I want him to be my mate.

I back away from Mateo, just a little bit, and I walk over to my bed and sit down. I need to breathe because Mateo is intense. Maybe even more intense than Tucker.

"I suppose I should call my dad and tell him." Mateo watches me as I sit down beside Tucker. I do keep space between us. As much I love touching them, it's very overwhelming.

"Maybe you should wait," Tucker speaks up.

I look over at him, curious as to why he's telling Mateo to wait to tell his father about me.

"Word is going to get out that the alpha's son met his mate. I'd rather my dad hear it from me than anybody else," Mateo says.

My mouth falls open.

His *dad* is the alpha?

I shake my head. "I can't be your mate."

His eyes snap to mine. "What? Why?"

I hold out my arms, motioning to my body. "Look at me. I'm the runt, Mateo. I can't be an alpha's mate."

"Clearly fate disagrees, because you *are* my mate." Mateo crosses his arms over his chest. "And if you don't stop saying stuff like that about yourself, we're going to have a problem."

I sigh, lowering my head. "When will the two of you see me for what I am—a runt?"

"I didn't mean for you to wait because of Layla. I just meant maybe you should wait because your dad is the freaking alpha. You know what will happen when he finds out. All the alphas will have to come meet her, and there will be a party in her honor." Tucker growls, turning to me. "I never meant for you to think that you're not strong enough. I don't give a damn what your pride thinks of you. You are *not* a runt, and I better not hear you call yourself that again or we are going to have problems."

"I think maybe I should call *her* alpha and have a word with him." Mateo crosses his arms over his chest, narrowing his eyes. "The bears like to mind our own business, but I think maybe it's time we do something about that guy."

62

I shake my head, standing up. "No, I promise it's fine. Alpha George barely even talks to me, let alone notices me. He beats the others often, but he's only beat me a couple of times. He says I'm too weak to even bother with."

My skin erupts in chills, and the hair on the back of my neck stands up. I glance over at Tucker in time to see him shred out of his clothes as he transforms into his wolf.

Holy crap. His wolf is *huge*, like almost to my chest on all fours.

Any bravery I was feigning is now gone, because I am terrified. I inch away from him slowly, until my back hits the wall.

"If you're going to kill me, just do it quick." I tense up, closing my eyes. I wait for him to pounce on me and attack, but nothing happens. Bravely, I open one eye to look.

Tucker's wolf is no longer there. Instead, he is in his human form, and he is *naked*.

My eyes widen in shock as I stare at him. And I *know* I should look away, but I just can't make myself close my eyes.

Being a shifter, I shouldn't be a stranger to nudity, but my alpha would never allow me to run with the rest of my pride. He didn't think I was worthy to run with the rest of them. So I have *never* seen a naked man before, and I am completely and utterly shocked.

"I think she's in shock." Mateo smirks.

"I've... never... seen a naked man before," I admit, my voice coming out as just a whisper.

Both Mateo and Tucker whip their head toward me, their mouths hanging open in complete shock.

"How?" Mateo asks.

I don't want to answer. If I tell them that my alpha didn't let me run with the rest of my pride, it will only make them hate Alpha George more. I don't want that. I don't want them to attack my pride, no matter how awful they think that they were to me.

Part of me always knew that what my alpha did wasn't normal. I knew that not everybody is as cruel as he is. But I never wanted to admit it to myself. He's my alpha. He's the leader of my pride. He is... somebody a lot of other panther shifters look up to. It's hard to think that maybe he's not a very nice guy.

"I should put some clothes on," Tucker says.

I nod.

He probably should.

But is it bad that I kind of don't want him to?

# The weird one.

Tucker, Mateo, and I spend the rest of our morning talking. Tucker catches Mateo up on a few things. Some things make me feel uncomfortable while they're talking, but I'm glad Tucker is telling him and not me.

One of the things Tucker tells Mateo is that I've never been kissed, and he tells him that he was the first person to ever hug me. Mateo just sits in stunned silence while Tucker reveals all that he knows of me, and every once in a while, Mateo's eyes flash black as his bear comes close to the surface.

Why do these guys feel the need to stand up for me like they do? I just don't get it. Nobody has ever looked out for me like this. But I am glad that I have them.

There is still a lot we need to discuss, like the fact that I have two mates instead of one, but we don't talk about that just yet.

After Tucker catches Mateo up to speed on everything that has happened since he picked me up on the side of the road in Key West, it's lunch time. I didn't have breakfast today, so I am starving by the time we make it into the dining hall, but I nearly lose my appetite when we walk in. The dining hall is half full, and it goes completely silent as everybody turns to look at Tucker, Mateo, and me.

I scoot over, hiding behind Mateo, but he grabs my hand, not letting me hide. Tucker grabs onto my other hand as we begin to walk through the dining hall toward the kitchen to get our food. Even though I am scared, they make me feel brave.

On our way, we walk past the table where the other members of my pride are sitting. They snarl their teeth at us as we pass. I dart a glance between Tucker and Mateo, wondering what they will do, but they don't even react. They act as if my pride doesn't even exist. I *wish* I could do that. I look back at my pride, and they stare at me in disgust. They've always done that, so it's nothing new.

Mateo squeezes my hand, so I look away from my pride. He smiles at me, and my pride is completely forgotten.

I wish I had met Mateo and Tucker sooner. They make everything better. If only I had been allowed to come to Shifter Academy before now.

I know I shouldn't be angry at Alpha George, but I kind of am. I would *never* admit that to anybody, and I would definitely never say it out loud. But I think how much better my life could have been had I come here as a freshman.

I've never felt like I belonged in my pride, and now I get why. I was never meant to be part of the pride. I was meant for more. I was meant for... well, I'm not sure what yet, but I'm going to have fun figuring it out.

The selection of food in the cafeteria makes my jaw drop. There is so much to choose from.

I have never gotten my pick of food in the pride. I get the scraps, whatever is left over after everybody else eats. But here, I get to choose.

"For somebody so small, you look awfully excited about food," Mateo comments.

"There is so much food," I say, in complete awe, trying to look at the choices all at once.

There is everything from pizza and burgers to sushi and pasta. There are so many things I want to try, things I've never had, but for now, I want a burger and fries. Tucker and Mateo go with me to get in the burger line.

The lady behind the counter asks me how many burgers

The lady behind the counter asks me how many burgers I want when I tell her what I want, which seems odd until I hear Tucker ask for four cheeseburgers. *Four.* Where does he even put it? And when Mateo asks for burgers, he gets six. I look at my one burger on my tray, wondering if I'll even be able to finish it.

"Are you sure that's enough food?" Mateo eyes my tray as we sit down at an empty table.

I nod, looking at my mountain of fries. "More than enough."

I pick up my burger to take a bite, and I watch as Tucker begins to eat his. He finishes the thing in four bites.

I guess wolves eat a lot.

Mateo eats pretty similar to the way Tucker does. And I have no idea where they put the food. There isn't an ounce of fat on them. Then again, I know shifting burns a lot of calories.

I don't shift very often. When I do, I'm always alone. If Alpha George or my dad sees how small my panther is, it just reminds them of how much they hate me. It makes things worse. So I always sneak off to shift, but I can't do it very often. I hate that is has to be like that, but I don't know what else to do.

Maybe I will get to shift more while I'm here. Do packs and prides get to shift and run together on the island? My heart sinks as I realize there is no way my pride would allow me to run with them. If they did, it would probably just be so they could pick on me and try to attack me. I'd rather avoid *that*.

As we are eating, another tray plops down at the table. I look up and see Levi take a seat beside Tucker.

"Hey, Levi," I say, as he sits down.

He smiles broadly, like he's proud I remembered his name. "Hey, Layla."

I've decided that I like Levi. He's really sweet, and not at all scary like I first thought.

I don't know how I ever thought Levi wasn't nice to begin with. His blue eyes are so warm and inviting. They're as blue as the ocean.

Mateo growls at Levi.

I turn to Mateo, wondering *why* he's growling at the tiger shifter. Do they not get along?

"Eyes off my mate." Mateo's voice is deep and gruff, almost like his bear is the one telling Levi not to look at me.

Is Mateo... jealous?

I didn't think he was the jealous type. I've been holding hands with both him and Tucker this morning and he didn't seem jealous then. But maybe he is.

Oh, gosh. Am I going to have to choose between Tucker and Mateo? It's something I haven't even thought about, but it makes sense. Shifters don't just have multiple mates, except the dragons. But most shifters, especially wolves and bears, are too possessive to share.

Levi looks at Tucker, his brow furrowed. "Wait, I thought Layla was your mate."

"She is." Tucker shrugs. "She's also Mateo's mate."

It's strange, truly. But then again, when has anything about me ever been 'normal'?

I am the only person in my pride shorter than 5'9". I'm the only one with strawberry blonde hair; everybody else has black hair. Nothing about me is like the rest of them.

"If we are going to discuss this, we should discuss it elsewhere." Mateo's voice is harsh.

I look up to see what he's talking about.

The entire cafeteria is quiet, and they're all looking our way, like they're trying to hear our conversation. I guess I can't blame them. It's a big deal that a panther walked into the cafeteria holding hands with a wolf and a bear. And now a tiger is sitting at our table.

Shifters are all cordial with each other, but we don't hang out. I thought *maybe* it was normal at Shifter Academy for different species to do so, because I saw them talking in the common room earlier, but when I look at the tables, I realize it's not. Wolves sit together, tigers are together, bears, ravens, all of them. Even though we are all in one room, we all still stick to our own kind.

I'm a little disappointed. I thought that Shifter Academy was about unity, but it's not. And I see now why. Because the first time different species sit together like this, it's a big deal. People stare and try to cause a scene.

I look at Levi's food and see that he has an entire pizza.

My eyes widen. "Can I have a slice?"

He grins, pushing the box my way. "Sure."

I try to ignore the looks we are getting, and focus on the new friends that I've made.

Well... more than friends, I suppose. But Levi is my friend. My first real friend. At least, I think he is.

"Hey, Levi, are we friends?" I take a huge bite of the slice of pizza he gave me. It's so good that I moan.

I've never tasted food so fabulous.

"We're friends." He glances at Mateo, probably to make sure he's not about to get mauled by a bear.

I smile. "Good. You are my first ever friend."

I notice Mateo stops glaring at Levi when I say that.

Maybe Levi really can be my friend. I would like that a lot.

I think I'm going to like Shifter Academy, even if I'm going to be the weird one here too.

# Four.

Mateo, Tucker, Levi, and I go to the common room after lunch to hang out for a while. Part of me wants to run back to my room and hide, but I remind myself that this school has been my dream since I was a kid. I'm not going to spend my time here hiding, not when I could be enjoying it.

Mateo does seem to be less possessive toward me when it comes to Levi now, but he still growls if Levi gets too close. He doesn't do the same whenever Tucker is close, so maybe there is hope for me to be with them both.

My fear is that I will have to choose between Tucker and Mateo, and just *thinking* about it makes me feel sick to my stomach with fear and anticipation.

How could I choose?

But another thought enters my mind, and that is what would being mated to two shifters be like? Is it even possible for me to merge my soul with two people? And I know I am naive, but I understand how sex works. Would one just watch while I mated with the other and vice versa?

I have so many questions, but I'm too scared to ask them.

As we're sitting there, I stiffen as a couple of guys from my pride approach us.

I know these guys, and they are bullies through and through.

Jack is the leader of the three bullies. He comes and stands in the front, his arms crossed over his chest.

He's all talk, no action. It's Brady that I'm worried about behind him. Brady likes to watch people bleed. He scares a lot of people in the pride. And Craig, who stands beside him, is his accomplice.

I don't look at the rest of them, because whenever I do, they like to punish me. I'd rather save myself from getting slapped across the face today.

"Was it not bad enough that you were hanging out with a bear and a wolf, but now you're hanging out with our sworn enemy?" Jack's voice is condescending and cruel. I don't have to look at him to know that he's staring at me with disgust. I've seen the look so many times I practically have it memorized. It's nothing new.

I hear Brady crack his knuckles from behind Jack, and I know he's antsy, wanting to fight somebody. He doesn't care who. He would even fight his friends.

I've never been on the other end of one of Brady's beatings, but I've seen the outcome many times. Even though shifters heal super fast, it took one boy in our pride three days to heal from what Brady did to him. And the alpha didn't even punish Brady, he just patted him on the back, like he was *proud* of him.

"I'm the sworn enemy?" Levi's mouth falls open in mock surprise.

Of course he knows that panthers hate tigers. It's why I reacted the way I did to him this morning on the boat. I was scared that he would attack me. Now that I'm here, it's clear to see that our rivalry is one sided. The tigers couldn't care less about us.

"Shut it, tiger scum," one of the panthers calls out from the back.

My stomach is in complete knots as I watch this play out. I know it's not going to end well.

"Don't talk about my friend that way." I'm not sure who is more surprised at the words that came out of my mouth, my pride or me. But we are all shocked.

I'm Layla. The soft spoken runt that never causes a problem, at least not on purpose. I try to not be seen.

Jack pulls his hand back, and I think he's about to smack me on my face, but Mateo stands up, moving into position between Jack and me.

I can't see Jack's face anymore, but I can see his feet. He backs up whenever Mateo growls at him. I'm not surprised. But I am surprised that Brady backs up too. Maybe it's because Mateo is a good eight inches taller than all of them.

I don't know why, but seeing my pride back up in fear makes me happy. For them to feel just a touch of what I have felt my entire life is incredible.

Every single day, I have lived in fear because of them, but not today. Today, I know that I am safe. Mateo and Tucker won't let anything happen to me. Heck, even Levi won't.

"Touch my mate and I will rip your arms from your body." Mateo growls out the threat.

"Mate?" The question echoes through the panthers.

"She's mine. Do you have a problem with that?" Mateo isn't asking because he cares what my pride thinks. He's asking because if they do have a problem with it, he is going to do something about it.

But, as always, Brady doesn't know when to stop. Not even when his opponent is bigger and stronger; he wants to fight. He takes a step toward Mateo, and that is all the encouragement my pride needs. They attack.

I stand there, not knowing what to do. Do I jump in? But what good would I do in a fight? I don't *need* to jump in though. Mateo, Tucker, and Levi can hold their own in a fight. Even against ten panthers at once, they don't seem to be struggling. I stumble backward in shock as I watch the fight unfold.

A panther advances on me, but I feel a hand on my arm.

*Mine*, my panther shouts at me.

A boy that I have never seen before steps in front of me and shoots white light from his hands, knocking the panther back about twenty feet.

He turns to me, raising an eyebrow. "You're my mate."

What?

*Three* mates?

I have *three* mates?

How is that even possible?

Yet, there is no denying it, because I can feel it deep in my soul, just like I can with Mateo and Tucker.

The boy is small, like me. He's about an inch taller than me, but he's way more badass. He turns to the panthers, who are still fighting against Mateo, Tucker, and Levi. He sends out a single blast of white light that knocks all the panthers back. When they look at who knocked them back, I expect them to attack, but they don't. Instead, they turn and *run*.

I've never seen my pack run from anything, yet they are scared of this small guy.

Mateo, Tucker, and Levi all turn to face him.

I still don't know the guy's name, but he tilts his head to the side and looks at my two mates and my friend. "Huh. It looks like the four of us share a mate."

"The four of us?" Levi raises an eyebrow.

The boy nods. "Yes."

Four? Does he think that Levi is my mate too?

Quicker than I thought possible, Levi appears in front of me, and he gently reaches toward me, grabbing my hand. When our skin touches, I feel a sense of... wholeness. I feel complete. And I *know* that he is mine too. All four of them are.

But why? And how?

The four of us stand there, staring at each other in stunned silence.

"Maybe we should take this somewhere private," the small guy suggests.

I have no idea what is going on, but I have four mates.

*Four.*

This is so weird.

# Alpha challenge.

I sit on my bed, my back resting against the headboard. I have my knees pulled up to my chest, hugging them, and my head resting on my knees.

Mateo paces back and forth, looking my way every once in a while. Tucker is just lying on my bed, his hands behind his head, gazing at the ceiling. Levi sits on my desk chair, his eyes trained on me. I don't think he's looked away since he found out that I'm his mate. And the small boy, who I have since realized is fae, is sitting crisscross on the bed. His purple eyes keep changing colors, and I *think* they change colors with his mood, but I don't know what each color means. Purple, pink, blue—those are the colors they keep flashing between. Pink when he looks at me.

"What is your name?" I speak, breaking the silence.

His eyes widen, like he's just now realizing he hasn't told me. "I'm Kai Bennett. What is your name?"

"Layla Rosewood." I tuck a piece of hair behind my ear. "I'm a panther shifter."

As if that wasn't already obvious. That's why the panthers tried to attack us to begin with, because they didn't like that I was talking to a tiger shifter.

Mateo stops pacing and walks closer to the bed. He sits on the very edge of it, looking between me and the rest of the guys. "So... your pack... they don't like you, do they?"

I lower my head, shaking it. "My pride doesn't like me, no. Because I'm—"

Tucker cuts me off. "Don't call yourself a runt."

I look up, smirking. "Because I'm *small*. Even my panther is tiny, and so I make the rest of my pride look weak. It's why I wasn't allowed to come to Shifter Academy before now."

Tucker begins to explain to Kai and Levi everything that happened, just as he did for Mateo earlier. I sit back and listen, surprised that Kai and Levi react similarly to how Mateo did earlier. It's weird to have people on my side for once.

Whenever Tucker tells them that I rode a bus all the way here, Kai turns to me. "Why didn't you just ride with the rest of your pack... or pride... whatever they are?"

"I tried. They didn't want me to ride with them. I think they were embarrassed to be seen with me." I pull my arms tighter, trying to make myself smaller. I want to hide, but I don't think my mates would let me do that.

Kai's eyes turn grey, then black, and he processes what I told him. "That is the most ridiculous thing I've ever heard. Your pride is your family. They should accept you for who you are, and not judge you because you're small and they think you're weak."

I shrug, not wanting to make a big deal out of it.

I am used to being ignored. But the guys... this is new for them. And I get why they are upset on my behalf, but it's really not a big deal. It's just my life.

"It doesn't matter now." I chew on the side of my lip, getting up the nerve to look at them again. "You four are kind of like my family now, right? I mean, we're kind of a pride. Or a pack. I don't care what it's called. I'm just not alone anymore."

Levi, who still hasn't taken his eyes off of me, gets up from the desk chair and walks over to the bed. He sits down beside me, grabbing my hand. "We are a family now. And it doesn't matter if your pride accepts you, because I know my pride will accept you."

"So will my pack." Tucker sits up and looks over at me. "I've already talked to my alpha, and he has given me his blessing."

He has?

When?

"I haven't spoken to my alpha yet, as I haven't had time," Mateo admits. "But I am calling him later today. It's a big deal. He will want to come to school and meet you."

"The fae are accepting of everyone." Kai's eyes turn blue. "Our queen is half wolf, so I know she won't have a problem with you."

I look down at my clothes, realizing that the girl who lent me clothes is the freaking fairy queen. My eyes widen.

She was so nice.

I'm not used to Alphas being nice, but maybe it is possible.

"The others of my pride will tell my alpha about all that has happened." My heart feels heavy. "He isn't going to be happy about it. I wouldn't be surprised if he came here to punish me."

"Punish you?" Levi seems genuinely confused.

"You know." I chew on my nail. "He'll want to make an example of me to the other panthers. He'll beat me. Since this is such a big deal, he'll probably hit me until I pass out."

It's going to be bad.

But certainly Alpha knows that I don't have control over who my mates are. Fate decides.

Still... I know Alpha George. He will somehow think that I was the one to cause this. He will think I did it on purpose. And he will not be happy.

"That's not happening." Mateo growls out the words, and his eyes are black.

I would think he doesn't have good control over his bear, but I think he probably has better control than most. He never shifts, even though his bear is always close to the surface.

"What are you going to do?" I shrug my shoulders, like it's not a big deal. "He's my alpha. He can do what he wants."

"When he gets here, I will issue an alpha challenge for you."

An alpha challenge is when one alpha fights for the right to steal a member of the other's pack or pride. It *never* happens, because most want to stay with their own kind. The fact that Mateo is even suggesting it is blowing my mind.

"Isn't it a fight to the death?" Tucker stutters over his words as he stares at Mateo.

Mateo shrugs. "Or until the other calls for mercy."

I shake my head. "No. I know my alpha. It doesn't matter if you call for mercy. If he pins you, he will kill you."

He grins. "Then I guess I better not get pinned."

I don't like this. Not at all. But what else can we do? My alpha will not let me go any other way. Even though he hates me, he is way too prideful to ever let a member of the pride go.

"Mateo, I don't want you to get hurt." Or worse. But I can't seem to make myself even consider the 'worse.'

"Don't worry, Layla. I am strong." He holds up his arm, showing me his muscle. "I'm made of steel."

I end up laughing, but I quickly let the smile fall from my face. "You don't get it, Mateo. My alpha might not be as strong as you, but he is fast, he is sneaky, and he's not above cheating."

"I've got this," he assures me.

But I'm still worried.

I just met Mateo. I can't lose him now.

# Out of control.

Everything feels so out of control right now.

I have four mates.

All four of my mates are different species.

That's insane, right?

And Mateo is planning on fighting my alpha, which I also have no control over. And I get why he wants to fight Alpha George. He really has to do this if I am ever going to be free of my pride, but it still scares me.

Now, we will just be playing a waiting game, wondering when my alpha will show up. And he *will* show. I just don't know if it'll be tomorrow or next week or even next month. But I know it's going to happen, and when it does, Mateo will be issuing the alpha challenge.

I have so much on my mind, but one of the things at the forefront is me worrying about the fact that I have four mates. How does that even work? It was bad enough thinking about it when I thought I just had two mates, but *four?*

Kai sits down beside me on the bed. Mateo, Tucker, and Levi are all sitting on the couch, watching a silly show on TV. But I just can't focus on it.

"What are you thinking so hard about?" Kai bumps his shoulder against mine.

I sigh, looking at him. "I'm just worried about everything."

"Like what?" he asks.

"The alpha fight." That one is pretty obvious.

He nods. "It is scary, but you have to trust that your mate knows what he's doing. He's strong. And he's your protector. If I could challenge your alpha, I would too."

My eyes widen at that.

Alpha George would die of embarrassment if he lost a fight to a guy as small as Kai. And I imagine Alpha George would lose, because Kai is incredible. He took on ten panthers at once like it was nothing.

"There is something else bothering you, though. I can feel it." He puts his hand on my knee. "You can talk to me. I'm a good listener."

It doesn't surprise me that Kai can feel my emotions. It's usually something that mates can do once they complete the mate bond, but from what I understand, fae are really good at reading others' emotions.

I take a deep breath, turning to face him. His eyes are purple right now, which I think is just the natural color of his eyes.

"Why do I have four mates?" Once I ask the question, all of my thoughts just come rushing out of my mouth. "And how does it even work? Do I choose one of you? Do you all just have to share me? Do all of you even *want* to be with me?"

Kai's eyes turn blue and he chuckles. "That's a lot of questions."

"Sorry. I just..." I'm curious. And worried. And very much freaking out. "I don't know how this all works, and I'm trying to figure it out. Panthers don't share mates, and we also don't have mates that aren't the same species. This isn't something I've learned about."

"While it's not common for shifters to share mates, it's not unheard of." Kai squeezes my thigh with his hand, and it's comforting. "My queen actually has four mates."

I nod. "I knew that."

Levi sits down on the bed in front of me. I didn't even realize he had gotten up from the couch. But then again, he is a tiger shifter, and cat shifters are very agile and sneaky. Not on purpose, but by design.

"There is a girl in my pride who has three mates as well," Levi informs me. "It's really not so strange to me. I see her with them all the time."

I didn't know that.

Tucker sits down on the other side of Levi. "My alpha's son is the fairy queen's mate, and he shares his mate with three other members from the pack, so I'm used to seeing it as well. It doesn't bother me."

Mateo is the last to sit on the bed. "The bears don't have a history of sharing mates, but for some reason, I'm not jealous or possessive when it comes to your other mates. It's strange, because bears are super possessive."

"So are wolves." Tucker shrugs his shoulders. "But I don't mind sharing you with the others."

I am relieved at their words. "So I don't have to choose?"

"No," Kai answers. His eyes are pink. "We are all yours."

How do I, the runt of the pride, deserve four mates? It doesn't seem real. Or fair.

I wonder if they will change their mind. So far, I have barely even touched them. What will happen when I decide to kiss them, or even more? But I suppose those are things I won't know until the time comes. Until then, I'm going to enjoy getting to know my mates.

For the first time in my life, somebody isn't disgusted by how small or weak I am. And not because they like me in spite of being small. They like me, period. And it completely blows my mind.

I will never get used to this.

# Too comfortable.

The rest of the day passes in a blur. An utter, complete, blur.

Everything that happened almost feels like a dream, from the time I got my letter, until I arrived here.

Well, other than my father slapping me against a wall, my shoulder being dislocated, and having to spend fifteen hours on a bus. If it weren't for those things, I am not sure I would believe this at all.

Whenever it's time for bed, Mateo decides that he's not leaving me alone all night. Which means Tucker, Kai, and Levi also aren't leaving. Thankfully the room has a lot of space. They end up getting four cots, spreading them around the room.

I feel bad that they have to sleep on cots. Mateo's feet hang off the thing by a good six inches. I try to at least get him to switch beds with me, but he refuses.

So that is how I ended up on a huge bed all by myself. I roll over, trying to get comfortable, but that's the problem. This bed is *way* too comfortable.

The mattress I have at home is well worn and hard. There is actually a spring sticking out of the top, and I cut myself on it at least once a week. This bed that I'm sleeping on now is new. And it's so fluffy. I can't help but feel like I don't deserve this.

Even after an hour, when all my mates are sound asleep, I stare up at the ceiling. There is no way I am going to sleep.

The cots don't look so bad.

I roll out of bed, walking carefully on the floor so I don't make a noise.

One advantage that a panther has over a bigger shifter is that we can sneak up on them. If it were a bear, you'd hear them coming from miles away. But the fact that I'm small makes me extra sneaky and quiet, something I perfected early in life. I found out that if I didn't draw attention to myself, most people wouldn't notice me. So I did just that. And it makes my life in the pride so much easier.

I study the cots. Mateo takes up the whole thing, and then some. Tucker and Levi nearly take up the whole space. But then I see Kai. He's about my size, and he's curled up on his side. I'm not sure what I'm thinking when I climb into his cot beside him, but now that I've made the decision, I am happy that I did. His is so comfortable, and he is so warm. The bed sucks, just like I thought it would.

Kai rolls over, opening one eye to look at me. I tense up, hoping he doesn't mind that I'm lying with him. To my surprise, he puts his arm around me and tugs me against him, holding me tight.

"I couldn't sleep," I whisper, wanting to explain it to him. I don't want him to be mad at me, but I don't think he is.

"Me either," he admits. "I just kept thinking about you, and how I wish I could hold you while I slept."

My eyes widen.

He really thought that about *me?*

"I feel... alive when I'm with you." I'm not sure where my bravery is coming from, but I feel a desperate need to tell him how I feel. "I've never felt... wanted, or desired. I've spent my entire life being the pride member that everybody hated. When we were kids, the others used to walk at least ten feet from me because they said I had cooties. And as we got older, it didn't get any better. I longed for the days when they would avoid touching me. Because when they did touch me, it was always to hit me, or knock me down. I used to keep count of how many bones had been broken on my body, but I lost count at one hundred and seven."

His grip tightens, and I feel his lips against my hairline. He kisses me so gently, and I didn't realize it was possible to touch somebody so softly.

"You will never have to go through that again," he promises. "Mateo will do the alpha challenge, and then you will be part of a new pack. One that won't abuse you."

I nod.

He's right.

That's going to be great.

But... I worry so much about Mateo. I don't want anything to happen to him because of me. I can't even let myself think about the possibility of him not winning.

"I've always been fascinated with fairies." I lay my head against his chest, loving the sound of his heart beating. I fit against him so perfectly. "Because they're small, like me. I used to imagine my mom was a fairy, and that she would come rescue me someday."

"What is your mom like?" He rubs his hand on my back, drawing circles with his thumb. His touch is so gentle and soft, like he's scared he's going to break me. But I'm a panther. We're stronger than that.

"I don't know. I never met her," I admit. "Anytime I would bring her up to my dad, he would backhand me. I eventually stopped asking."

"I'm sorry for all that you've had to go through, Layla."

I peer up at him, smiling. "I'm not. Everything that happened led me here, and I don't regret that."

Kai leans down and kisses my forehead. "Let's go to sleep. We'll need our rest for tomorrow."

"Good night, Kai."

"Night, Layla."

I put my head against his chest again, listening to his heart beating. I don't think I'll be able to sleep at all, but his heart slowly lulls me into a deep slumber.

# Sunday, August 23
# Beautiful.

I wake up with the feeling that somebody is looking at me. I'm scared to open my eyes, scared that somebody from my pride has decided to come pick on me this morning, but then I remember... Shifter Academy... I'm not at home.

I open my eyes and find that Mateo, Tucker, and Levi are standing over me, their mouths hanging open in shock. And somebody has their arms around me. Kai, I realize.

My face grows warm as I remember the previous night. I couldn't sleep, so I climbed into bed with Kai.

Well, this is slightly awkward.

"The bed was too comfortable." I want them to know that it was me who moved to this bed completely on my own accord. The last thing I want is for them to be mad at Kai. Or jealous, which is my fear in all of this. "And I couldn't sleep. Kai was the only one who had enough room."

Mateo chuckles.

I feel relief at his response, because out of everybody, I was the most worried about him being jealous. I know that Kai is strong, but Mateo is more than twice his size.

"Can it be my turn to cuddle you tonight?" Tucker raises a hand, like he's waiting on a teacher to call on him.

I shrug. "I don't mind. That bed is too big for just me. I couldn't sleep there knowing that you guys were on cots."

Levi, who is standing the closest to me, reaches out and touches the side of my face. "You are far too beautiful in the morning."

I'm certain that I am blushing from his words.

I'm the opposite of beautiful right now. My strawberry blonde hair is always messy in the mornings, and I'm certain it's sticking up all over the place. But even if my hair was fixed, I'm not considered beautiful. As my pride has reminded me many times in my life, I am ugly.

"You don't believe me." He cocks his head, studying me.

How can he read me so easily?

Still, I won't deny it.

I shake my head.

Levi calls me beautiful because he's my mate. He's *supposed* to think that. And maybe he truly does believe it. But I know that I'm not.

"Why do you think you're not beautiful? That's absurd." Matco shakes his head, narrowing his eyes. He genuinely appears confused.

My mouth opens, but it takes me a few seconds to articulate the words. "I have been told my whole life, almost every single day, just how ugly I am. I've been told how horrible it will be for my mate to have to look at me, and that it would be better for me to wear a bag over my head while I'm... mating." My face grows warm at the mention of 'mating.' "So, that is why I know I'm not beautiful."

Tucker and Mateo both growl at my words. Levi reaches his hand forward again, stroking my cheek. "Your pride lied to you, Layla."

I shake my head, sitting up in the cot. "No, Levi. You don't get it. You only think I'm beautiful because of this bond. If it wasn't for these supernatural feelings, you would think I'm ugly too."

"I was attracted to you before I knew you were my mate," Levi admits. "And I felt so guilty when I found out that Tucker was your mate, because it didn't lessen my attraction to you. I was lusting after somebody who I thought could never be mine. So, it's not just these supernatural feelings. And I'm sorry that your pride ever made you feel anything but the most beautiful girl on the planet, because that is what you are."

My heart swells at his words.

He means them.

And I don't even know what to think about it.

Maybe...

Maybe the panthers thought I was ugly because I don't look like them. They all have black hair, except for me. Maybe panthers don't like strawberry blonde hair. And where their skin is pale, mine turns golden every summer. Maybe it's possible that other species *are* attracted to me.

But it doesn't matter what anybody else thinks, because my mates are attracted to me. Which is more than I could've ever dreamed of.

I never wanted to meet my mate. I imagined he would be as cruel as the rest of the panthers. I thought he *would* be a panther. But I'm so happy to know that my mates are different from my pride. And I feel so guilty for thinking that about them, but I can't help it. My pride has been nothing but cruel to me, and I'm so glad that I'm away from their abuse.

Maybe it is possible for me to be happy.

Kai stirs beside me, stretching out. He grins as he opens his eyes and sees me. "Good morning, beautiful."

There is that word again.

Beautiful.

Except this time, I'm not going to argue with him about it.

My stomach growls. I put a hand against it.

"Let's go get breakfast." Mateo doesn't ask. He demands. I think that's one of the things I like about him.

He is the future alpha, so I suppose he doesn't *have* to ask.

"What he means to say is, would you like to get breakfast?" Tucker glares at Mateo. "You can't go all alpha on our mate."

I laugh.

One thing is certain—life will never get boring with these four.

# Eat.

The panthers glare at me in the dining hall, but none of them make a move to come toward us. It seems that Kai has thoroughly scared them away.

I know I shouldn't feel as elated as I do. I shouldn't rejoice in the fact that my pride is terrified. But I can't help it. They sort of deserve it after the way they've treated me. Soon, I won't be part of their pride. I will be in Mateo's pack.

I almost feel sorry for the members of my pride. I hate that they're stuck with Alpha George forever, unless somebody *actually* decides to fight him, which I doubt they will.

Alpha George is scary. I've heard the stories of people who have tried to fight him before, but they always lose. And they *die*.

My alpha doesn't offer second chances, which is what scares me so much about Mateo fighting him. What if Mateo loses? The thought scares the crap out of me. And if he does lose, if Alpha George kills him, I know without a doubt that he will do the same thing to me. He will want to make an example of me. Not only to the other panthers, but to the other alphas.

Alpha George hates Shifter Academy. That much he has said since I can remember. He talks about how shifters should stay with their own kind, and he says that peace is just an illusion. He thinks it's only a matter of time before war breaks out, but he doesn't seem horrified by the idea. He seems excited. He *wants* there to be war.

My alpha is blood thirsty. And I've always known that, but now that I have a chance to possibly break away from the pride and join a different pack, I feel like I can see clearer than I ever have before. And I see that Alpha George is not a good alpha. He rules with fear, and that's not how a pride is supposed to be ran.

Kai turns and looks at my pride. When he does, his eyes turn white—not completely so. There is still a dark purple outline, and flecks of lighter purple throughout his eye. I see sparks come out of his fingers, and the rest of my pride must see it too, because they look away.

My jaw drops open.

I knew they were terrified, but to show it in front of the other shifters? That is very unlike them.

Kai looks at me, his eyes turning from white to pink. "They shouldn't bother you anymore."

I grin, but I'm still worried. Kai doesn't know my pride. He doesn't know what they are capable of, and what they would be willing to do to me, what they *have* done to me.

The truth is, my mates can't always be around. Tomorrow, we will be going to class. And I *know* that I can't be in every single class with them.

All the time I spent dreaming about coming to Shifter Academy, I never once realized the hell that would await me. Shifter Academy isn't a break from my pride. It's just me being locked in classrooms with them. It's me being trapped on a freaking island with them. There is no escaping.

I am doomed.

"Eat." Mateo pushes my tray closer to me.

I turn away from my pride and begin to eat, even though I seem to have lost my appetite. After seeing how much Mateo freaked out over the fact that I only ate *one* cheeseburger, I can't imagine how furious he would be if I didn't finish my breakfast.

"You've got to start eating more." Tucker shakes his head, looking at my one breakfast sandwich.

I shrug. "This will fill me up."

"Only because you've been starved your whole life," Mateo grumbles.

"I have to agree with them," Kai says.

I raise an eyebrow at him, looking at his plate. He also just has one breakfast sandwich, so it doesn't seem fair that he's judging me for eating the same amount as him.

"I'm not a shifter." His eyes are purple as he explains. "So my diet is pretty small. But you burn a lot of calories when you shift into your panther. I'm surprised you even have enough energy to call on your animal. You probably sleep for days after a shift."

I tilt my head to the side.

How did he know?

I always thought it was because I was weak. That is what my dad told me. But what he's saying kind of makes sense.

Mateo puts one of his six sandwiches on my plate. "Eat."

"Maybe eat one and a half," Kai suggests. "You don't want to suddenly start doubling what you ate before. Work up to it, and let your stomach stretch out."

"The clothes she has on belong to Penelope." Tucker shakes his head. "I should've realized. Penelope is a lot shorter than Layla. If her clothes fit her, then she's a lot underweight."

"Why is she wearing my queen's clothes?" Kai cocks his head.

My face grows warm at the conversation they're having.

Tucker turns to me, waiting for me to explain it to them, but I'm embarrassed.

So embarrassed.

How do I explain it to them?

"My clothes are hand me downs. And seeing as I am so small, I can't fit into most of the pride's clothes." I twirl my hair around my finger, trying to get up the nerve to spill it. "The clothes weren't so bad. They were just..."

I can't say it.

I can't.

"She was wearing clothes meant for a twelve-year-old," Tucker says for me. "If my mate wants to wear a t-shirt with a unicorn on it, I'm fine with it. But she didn't want to be wearing it."

He's right.

I didn't want to be wearing it.

The rainbows, the frilly skirts, the unicorns... they were cool, but they only made me stand out more. I want to blend in. And me wearing this dress that Penelope gave me helps me blend in.

"My mom is sending clothes to the school for her. They should be here tomorrow." Tucker looks at me. "You will have a lot to choose from, don't worry. And whatever you don't want, Mom will donate to charity."

His mother is so kind that it nearly brings tears to my eyes.

I wonder how my own mother was. Was she cruel, like the rest of the panthers? Or was she kind? Was she the kind of mom who would donate clothes to charity? Or would she throw them away so nobody else could use them?

Our pride does that. While I get the hand me downs that nobody can fit into anymore, they only do that so they don't have to buy me new clothes. But when the older ones are done with their clothes, they are thrown out. Just the thought breaks my heart. What if somebody else could use those clothes?

"Make sure you tell your mother thank you for me." My voice breaks as the words leave my mouth. I hope someday I can thank her in person.

"I will." Tucker reaches across the table and squeezes my hand. "You better eat."

It's a struggle to finish my one and a half breakfast sandwiches, but I do it. Mateo seems happy that I was able to eat as much as I did, but my stomach hurts from eating so much. I'm definitely not used to it.

My mates are going to take care of me. I just hope that someday I can return the favor.

# Fate thinks I'm good enough.

The library is my happy place.

Reading has been my only escape for as long as I can remember. While other members of the pride would rave about whatever show they were watching, I would be just as excited over a book I read.

Reading is how I would escape to other worlds. It's the only thing that kept me sane. And reading is what made me realize that maybe the members of my pride are just not good people.

I know that abuse isn't normal.

I know that my dad punching me into the wall is abuse.

But it is my life, at least it was, and I thought it was the only life I could ever have.

Shifters don't belong in the human world. If I had run away from my pride, that is all I would have. I would be frozen at my age, while everybody grew old around me. I'd have to keep moving. I'd never have real connections or real friends. At least with my pride, I knew they would stay young with me. Even if they hated me, they were my pride. My species. At least I had *that* in common with them.

When Kai and Tucker take me to the library later that morning, I am beyond thrilled.

I don't know how they knew about my love of reading. Perhaps it was the fact that my suitcase was only half full of clothes, the other half was stuffed with books—as many books as I could physically fit in the case.

I walk through the aisles, my fingers brushing against the spine of the books.

These books aren't like the ones I have. The ones I have were abused before they got to me. Some of them are missing pages. But not these books. These books are new and beautiful. The spines aren't bent back, and they are well taken care of.

I pick up a few, reading the description on the backs.

"What kind of books do you like?" Kai asks, as I put one back on the shelf.

"Uh..." My face grows warm. "Anything as long as there is romance in it."

Even though I didn't think I would ever find my mate, I always longed for love. I've wanted to be loved like a man loves a woman in a romance novel. I want to know what it feels like to be kissed in the rain. I want to know what it feels like to be so overcome with passion that I beg a man to ravish me. I want to know what it feels like to do the filthy things that they do.

"This one looks interesting." Tucker passes me a book. "It's about a vampire and a succubus that fall in love."

I frown, reading the blurb. "But they aren't mates. Someday, the vampire would find his mate and the succubus would be left alone. I don't like tragic romances."

Tucker takes book back from me. "Only happy endings, then."

"Oh, here's one." Kai holds a book in his hand. "It's about a wolf whose mate is a dragon."

My eyes grow wide.

That's kind of cool.

Dragons, like most shifters, rarely mate outside of their species. Whenever they do, we usually hear about it because it's such a big deal. It's considered an honor if you're mated to a dragon, because they are so special and rare.

Of course, being mated to a fae is also special, considering there are so few of them around.

I grab the book from him, thinking it sounds like something I would want to read.

"Oh, you should read this one." Tucker puts another book in my hand. "It's about a dragon who has five mates. Maybe it'll help you, considering you have four mates."

Oh, that does sound interesting.

I need all the help I can get when it comes to having multiple mates, because I don't know the first thing about being mated to one shifter, let alone four.

We continue to look through the library, but I don't grab any more books. I get the feeling that my mates are going to keep me too busy for reading, but maybe I can read while they watch TV or something.

As we walk into the next aisle, I hear somebody whisper shouting.

"Who does she think she is?" The girl complains. "She's not even a bear shifter, yet she thinks she can steal the attention of our future alpha."

Oh.

She is definitely talking about me.

"Mateo will grow bored of her quickly," another voice says, this one higher pitched. "I mean, look at her. She's got to be a virgin. Mateo is probably just using her. Alphas like girls who are untouched."

They both giggle, and I feel sick to my stomach.

Mateo isn't like that. I *know* he isn't. He would never use anybody for that.

Right?

I mean, they're not wrong about Alpha's liking virgins. A lot of the girls from my pride have lost their virginity to Alpha George. I've heard them talk about it. But that doesn't mean Mateo is like that.

Besides, Mateo is my mate. That means he's mine now. No matter what his pack thinks, you can't change fate.

But what if...

I mean, I have four mates. What if they decide I'm not enough for the four of them? They could get other girls. What right would I have to complain about it, seeing as they have to share me? It would be hypocritical to say anything.

"It's not true." Tucker shakes his head. "Mateo isn't like that. I know him. We've been friends since freshman year. I've never seen him go after any girl."

"Girls probably chase him." I frown at the idea.

"Yeah, but he can't help that," Tucker insists.

"He's probably been with a lot of virgins. A lot of girls." And I have no right to even be jealous, because it all happened before me.

"If you're worried about it, you should talk to him."

I look at Tucker and Kai. "What about the two of you? How many girls have you been with?"

"None," Tucker answers. "My alpha has a rule against it. And while he said he knows he can't stop anybody from dating, he asked if we would at least wait until after high school to be intimate with anybody. I respect my alpha, so I was waiting."

I'm relieved at his answer.

I look at Kai.

He glances between Tucker and I, tugging the neck of his shirt. "Um... well, there were two girls over the summer. But they didn't mean anything to me. And if I had known you existed, I never would have."

I'm being silly.

My mates were allowed to do whatever they wanted before we met. Nobody in my pride waits for their mate. One girl tried, but Alpha George took her virginity in front of the pride at a meeting one night, claiming that she was just too tempting.

I shiver to think what would've happened to me if the other members of my pride hadn't been so repulsed by me. Would my alpha have forced me to get down on all fours while he took me from behind with everybody watching? He even allowed a few members to take turns with her once he was done.

But Mateo isn't like my old alpha. He is kind and gentle. He would never force a girl to have sex with him. I know that just from the way he treats me.

"Those girls don't matter," I tell Kai.

His shoulders relax at my words. "Layla, I could live an entire millennium and never deserve you."

I shake my head. "It's me who doesn't deserve you."

I'm trash and I know it.

Those girl bears were right. Mateo does deserve a lot better than me. All my mates do. So I will spend my life trying to be enough for them. Because it doesn't matter what I or anybody else thinks. Fate chose me.

Fate thinks I'm good enough.

# Fight.

I don't see the two girls approaching our table at lunch until I hear their voices. It's not that they were being sneaky, it's just that I wasn't paying attention to them. I've been off in my own thoughts since that conversation with Kai and Tucker in the library.

I wonder what it was like to grow up in Tucker's pack. Or what it was like with the fae. What would it be like to have a pride that actually cares? Or even just family... or anybody, period. What did it feel like to not go to bed hungry or alone?

But all those thoughts are pushed aside when the tall blonde juts her chest out, fluttering her long eyelashes. "Hey, Mateo." She bends down a little bit, supposedly to get down to his level while he's sitting, but I know it's not that. The girl wants to give him an eyeful of her cleavage. Little does she know that she's giving every single person in the dining hall a show as well.

Gross.

I recognize the voice. She was one of the girls talking in the library. I know from hearing her conversation with her friend that she doesn't like me very much. The feeling is mutual.

Mateo doesn't even look up from his food. "What do you want, Angela?"

"Brittany and I were wondering if you wanted to hang out with us later." She doesn't seem put off by his grumpy tone. "Maybe alone in my room."

"Not interested." Mateo puts his arm around me, pulling me closer to him. "I'll be hanging out with my mate."

Angela looks at me, her dark brown eyes narrowed. But she quickly composes herself, putting the fake smile back in place. She reaches out to put her hand on Mateo.

Something in me snaps when I see her reaching for him. I jump up and grab her wrist before she can make contact.

"Touch him and I will kill you." The words are out of my mouth before I even have time to process them.

I would never kill somebody. Ever. But I'm also not going to back down from the threat. Mateo is my mate. How dare she think she can touch him.

"How is a runt like you going to kill me?" Angela grins at her insult.

She's right.

I am a runt.

There is no way I could take her on in a fight.

Angela stands at least six feet tall. Her friend Brittany, who is behind her, is nearly as tall. Between the two of them, I wouldn't stand a chance.

But as it turns out, I don't have to fight her. Because Mateo really hates that she just called me a runt. He knows that is what my pride used to call me as an insult.

Mateo growls, and both Angela and Brittany back up, their faces white as a ghost.

"Call my mate a runt again and you'll find yourself without a pack. Nobody disrespects the alpha's mate like that, you understand?"

I can *feel* the power behind his voice, and I know he's using an alpha command.

Angela and Brittany both nod vigorously.

"Good. Now don't let me see you again for the next week." His knuckles are white from making a fist so tight.

"Yes, Alpha." Angela and Brittany both take off running, their heads down.

Tucker laughs, clapping his hands. "That was beautiful."

I look over and see that my mates are all smiling.

"Beautiful the way you threatened her." Levi shakes his head. "Even I was scared."

I smile, feeling kind of proud of myself.

It was kind of brave, even if it was stupid. "There is no way I could've taken those girls in a fight."

"You don't even have to worry about fighting anybody." Mateo pushes me back to my seat.

"But I should learn how to fight," I think aloud. "I mean, I've always wanted to know how. I thought if I could fight, I would put the pride in their place."

"No." Mateo growls the words, his eyes shifting black. "You will not learn how to fight. It's my job as Alpha to take care of you."

It's one thing to feel his power directed at somebody else. It's another to have it directed at me.

I cower back, feeling dejected.

"If you wish to learn how to fight, I will teach you." Levi glares at Mateo as he says it, but his eyes soften when he looks at me. "Don't ever let anybody make you feel weak. If learning to fight is important to you, you should learn."

I want to tell him that it's not important. I don't want my mates to fight over this.

But it is important.

I nod. "I don't want to go against Mateo, but I want to learn."

"Then we will teach you." Tucker nods, like the conversation is final.

Mateo growls, jumping up from the table, and then he storms out of the dining hall.

My chest aches, because I know I hurt him.

"Don't worry, beautiful. He'll be back. He just needs to cool off." Kai slides into the seat where Mateo was sitting.

I hope he's right.

The absolute last thing I want is to hurt my mate.

# Teach me.

After lunch, I look for Mateo, but he doesn't come back to our room.

Well, I guess it's my room? I don't know. I think I'm supposed to share it with my mates, but they're waiting for me to be ready for the physical aspect of our relationship.

Most mates meet and complete their bond right away, at least within the first week of meeting. The thought of doing that, of having sex, it gives me butterflies.

I want to be physical with them. Even though I've just met them, I am so attracted to them. And last night when Kai was holding me, I wondered what it would be like if he moved his hand down a little farther and touched me.

But I'm scared to tell them that.

And right now, Mateo hates me.

I wonder if I should tell him that I changed my mind. I wonder if I should just give in and not learn how to fight. But to do that would be a dishonor to myself. I want to learn how to fight. It's something I've wanted all my life. Now that it's been offered to me, I can't turn it down. And if Mateo knew how important it was to me, he wouldn't ask it of me.

"Where is Mateo?" I ask Tucker, after I double check my room and make sure he's not in it.

"He just needed to cool off." Tucker grabs my hand. "Don't worry about it for now."

But I can't just let it go. "I need to talk to him. Can you please take me to him? It's important."

I have to fight for what I want. I have to tell my mates when there is something that I need for me. And that is why I don't want to wait to talk to Mateo. I need to explain it to him now.

Tucker nods when he sees that I am serious. "I will take you to him. I know where he goes when he's upset. But I have to walk you there."

I'm absolutely okay with him walking me there. In fact, I don't know if I'd want to go unless he walked me there. It's not really safe for me to be by myself right now. I don't think Angela and Brittany would attack me after what Mateo said, but you never know. But even without them as a threat, my pride would *love* the chance to get me alone. The thought of that terrifies me, so I will stick as close to my mates as I possibly can.

Tucker grabs my hand as we leave the room. Holding his hand is so comforting. I love how small my hand is in his, and I love the butterflies he gives me. This man is mine, and I still can't believe it.

We walk through the castle. Thankfully there aren't many people in the hallways or the entryway. I'm so sick of getting stared at. I'm surprised when we walk out the front door, but I shouldn't be. Mateo seems like the kind of guy who would like to get away outside.

"Will Mateo be mad that you're taking me to his secret spot?" I ask, as Tucker holds my hand, leading me away from the school.

He shakes his head. "Trust me, Mateo will be the opposite of mad."

I bite my lip, not sure if I really believe him. I mean... I'm invading Mateo's personal spot. It's where he goes to get away from everybody. And since I am the one he's mad at, he's going there to get away from me specifically.

When we get to this one section of the beach, there is an old tower that overlooks the ocean. It's not tall, maybe as tall as a lifeguard stand.

Tucker points up the stairs at the door, and then he turns around and leaves me there alone. I'm a little bit sad that he left me here by myself. I'm scared to talk to Mateo right now. But I've come this far. There's no turning back now.

I walk up the stairs, my heart racing, and then I open the door. I find Mateo sitting on the floor, gazing out the window. He looks up at me, cocking his head in confusion. I don't say anything. I just walk toward him and sit down on the floor beside him.

"Hey." I nod my head in greeting, like all is right in the world.

Mateo just turns his attention forward.

Yikes.

He really *is* mad at me.

"Can I explain why I want to learn how to fight? That way you can understand?" Tears press against the back of my eyes, but I refuse to let them fall.

I don't want Mateo to be mad at me. It hurts when he is.

Mateo looks at me, his dark brown eyes wide. I know he's willing to listen, but he's still so mad. But whatever he sees when he looks at me crumbles his resolve. He picks me up and sets me down in his lap, cuddling me to him.

I sigh, leaning into his embrace.

He feels so good.

But right now, I can't focus on those things. I have to tell him why it's so important for me to learn how to fight.

I take a deep breath before I begin. "Do you remember when I told you that I lost count of how many broken bones I have gotten after one hundred and seven?"

He nods, tensing up.

"The fact is, I don't know how many bones I broke the one hundred and seventh time. It was summer and the other kids liked to torture me. This older boy held me down while this girl who hated me kicked me and punched me. She broke my fingers one by one. And she beat me until I was so broken and bloody that I couldn't move. I stayed in the woods. I lay on the ground during a hurricane because I couldn't move. I was under a tree and I remember I was worried about it falling on top of me." I shake my head, trying to repel the memories.

Mateo grips his hand on my thigh, and he grits his teeth. I can tell he's upset, but I know it's important to explain this to him.

"I know that you are my protector." I put my hand on his forearm. "But I've never been able to protect myself. I've taken beating after beating from my pride. And I longed for the day I could fight back. I wanted to show them that the runt of the pride can be strong too. I want to learn how to fight for *me*. I know you can protect me, Mateo. Don't doubt that. But this isn't about you. I wish, for your sake, that I could let it go, but I can't. I've wanted this for so long."

He sighs, his eyes softening. "Layla..."

His voice breaks when he says my name, and that is when I know he understands. I just hate that I had to tell him everything that had happened to get him to understand.

I wanted to keep the worst of the abuse a secret. It's in the past. I have my mates. My old pride can't hurt me now. But if being open with Mateo will help him understand, that is what I'll do.

"Will you help teach me?" I peer up at him through my lashes. "Mateo, I don't want to do this without you."

He nods. "Yeah, Layla. I'll help you."

I put my arms around him, squeezing him. "Thank you."

He grumbles something, tightening his arms around me. And that is where we stay until almost dinner.

# Addicted.

When we get back to the room, Kai, Tucker, and Levi are all waiting there, anxiously. As soon as Mateo tells them that they are going to teach me to fight, I swear all three of them wear a matching smirk. I ask Kai about it, and he just tells me that I could talk Mateo into anything. Which I doubt. Mateo merely understands now why it's important to me.

I'm surprised that I'm hungry when we head to dinner. Since the guys found out that my pride was basically starving me, they've made it their mission to force feed me until I'm so stuffed I can barely move.

When Tucker carries a huge platter of burgers and fries to the table, I suck in a surprised breath. I feel like he has enough food to feed the entire dining hall. But then again, I'm pretty sure I saw Mateo eat six burgers yesterday like it was nothing, and then still go back for dessert.

I've never been able to shift without fainting afterward. And I know that's not normal. Not even close. But I wonder what it will be like to shift into my panther and feel invigorated when I shift back.

Soon, I will know.

I ignore the stares that I get from my pride. Them taunting me is just my lot in life, and I should just accept it for now. One more year and I won't have to put up with them anymore.

*If* Mateo wins.

He has to.

I told Mateo earlier that I trusted him to protect me, and that is still true. I have to trust him, even though I'm scared.

Kai, who is sitting to my right, shakes his head. "Shifters eat so much."

Levi shrugs, grabbing a burger from the pile. He stuffs half of it in his mouth.

I'm mated to animals, quite literally.

He sees me watching him. "What?" he asks around a mouth full of food.

Kai and I both bust out laughing.

I grab a burger from the pile, eating it like a normal person. Meanwhile, Mateo is already on burger number two before I take my second bite.

I watch in amazement as the pile of food slowly dwindles. I didn't think we were going to be able to eat it all, but I think we might.

"Eat another." Levi puts a burger on my plate as I finish up the first one.

I groan, putting a hand to my stomach. "I'm so full."

But I take a bite anyway.

In my mind, I know this is right. I know I should be eating more. I'm not getting near enough calories. But knowing doesn't help the fact that my stomach just isn't accustomed to eating so much food.

As I'm eating dinner, a boy approaches our table. I can smell that he's a wolf.

"Hey, Tucker. What's up?"

The boy looks about our age, probably eighteen. And he's smiling at Tucker, so I'm hoping that it's a good thing that he's here. Maybe this is Tucker's friend.

"Hey." Tucker nods. "What's going on?"

"The pack is having a party tonight, if you want to come." The boy glances up at the rest of us, then back at Tucker. "All of your friends are invited too. I think some bears are coming anyway. And the fae, of course."

Tucker shrugs. "Maybe."

A party?

I've never been to a party in my life. I've read about them, plenty of times. But in books, parties are usually just for drinking and doing drugs, all of which I am completely against, given that my father is an alcoholic.

The boy turns and walks away from the table, and then Tucker looks at the rest of us.

"It could be fun." He takes another bite of his burger.

Kai, Mateo, and Levi turn and focus on me.

Meaning that the decision is up to me.

I finish chewing the bite I just took and I swallow before answering. "I know that I don't have a right to ask anything of you guys. But please don't drink tonight."

Levi rubs the back of his head with his hand. "Layla, we don't drink. It's against the law. We're shifters. If we get drunk, we could seriously hurt somebody, or even accidentally reveal ourselves to humans. The alpha council outlawed it many *millennia's* ago. Like, nearly at the beginning of our existence. A few people have tried to fight it over the years, but it's stuck."

That makes sense. "Oh. I didn't know."

My pride doesn't follow that rule at all. My dad is a drunk, but other members of the pride are just as bad as him. Even our alpha gets wasted on Friday nights.

"Does your pride drink?" Mateo asks.

I nod my head, just once. But it's enough. "My dad... he can't get out of bed without the stuff."

Because we are shifters, it takes more to get us drunk. My dad can drink four bottles of whiskey a day like it's nothing. I know from reading human books that it's not normal to drink that much. It's not even normal for a shifter to drink that much. It makes him smell different, more like alcohol and less like a panther. It even affects his ability to shift, but he doesn't care, as long as he gets his next fix.

"Layla, you know we have to report it to the council, right?" Kai asks. "Because if we don't, we would be in a lot of trouble."

My mouth opens, then shuts.

I want to tell them to keep quiet, but part of me wants my dad to get help. Maybe this could be his wake up call.

"Will they help him?" I tuck a piece of hair behind my ear. "My dad... he can't resist it. He's addicted. Can they help him get off it?"

Kai puts his arm around me, pulling me against him. "You're too sweet for your own good."

"We'll get him help," Tucker promises.

And I believe them.

I nod. "Okay, then. You should tell the council."

I tell them the rest of it too.

About the alpha drinking, and all the rest of the pride members.

I always thought it was normal, but now that I know it's not... I'm relieved. I know more than anybody that alcohol can change a person, and I didn't want my mates to change. I like them the way they are.

# Throbbing.

I'm going to a party tonight. A wolf party at that.

I never thought I'd be invited to a party, much less go to one. I'm kind of excited to see what it's like. Maybe I will make friends while I'm there.

In the bag of clothes that Tucker's alpha's mate brought me, there was a curling iron and a hair straightener. I've never used either of those things, but I figure I'd give it a shot. I plug in the hair straightener because it seems the easiest to use.

I've seen other girls in my pride use a hair straightener. Living in Florida, it's pretty much a necessity with all the humidity. But I've always relied on hair ties to get me by during the summer months.

After the iron heats up, I run it over a chunk of my hair, amazed at how it changes.

My hair is naturally wavy. When I use the straightener, it not only takes out the wave, but it makes it shiny and somehow it even feels softer. I like it.

I continue running the straightener over my hair, until I've done my whole head. I'm surprised it didn't take that long either, maybe twenty minutes.

My hair is gorgeous. With my hair straight, it somehow brings out the blonde, making it look lighter. And it hangs down to my waist, not too much longer than it was before.

After fixing my hair, I realize I should probably hurry and finish getting ready. I can't just hog the bathroom. I have to share it with four other people. I know they don't have to fix their hair like I do, but they probably still need the bathroom.

I put on the dress I picked out earlier. It's a soft pink color. It fits me well, but it is a little short. It's still modest though, hitting me about the middle of my thigh.

I take a deep breath and walk out the door, wondering if the guys will even notice my hair. Will they think I look pretty?

The question of them noticing is answered right away.

Mateo and Tucker are watching TV. Levi is sitting on the bed, his phone in his hand, and Kai is lying beside him, just staring at the ceiling. All four of them turn when the door opens.

Mateo's eyes widen, as he slowly scans me from head to toe. Tucker has a smirk on his face, like he's proud. And maybe he is. Maybe he's proud that I am his. Levi drops his phone, but doesn't move to pick it up as his jaw drops too. But Kai... his reaction is by far my favorite. He sits up so fast he ends up falling out of the bed. I have no idea *how* it happened, but I can't stop laughing as I run over to check on him.

"Are you all right?" I bite my lip, trying to stop smiling, but I can't help it.

Tucker, Levi, and Mateo are all laughing. Hearing them laugh makes it harder for me not to, but I have to make sure he's not hurt.

"I'm fine." Kai pushes himself off the floor, coming to stand in front of me. "You are absurdly beautiful."

He leans closer, kissing me on the forehead so softly. All humor is forgotten.

My heart races. "Thanks."

I find myself wanting to pull Kai's lips to mine. I want to know what his lips would feel like pressed against mine. What would he taste like? What would his body feel like if he held me close and kissed me? But before I get the opportunity to, Levi bounces up beside Kai.

"Very beautiful," Levi says, agreeing with what Kai said.

Somehow, having the two of them stand before me does nothing to lessen my feelings. I still want to kiss Kai. And I also want to kiss Levi. I want both of their hands on me at the same time. And I know that it's possible from the books I've read. I read a little bit of the dragon book that Tucker picked out for me earlier, and I know that it's *very* possible to be with more than one guy at a time.

Kai's eyes are pink as he looks at me.

"What does pink mean?" I wonder aloud. I whisper the words, not wanting to break whatever it is that is going on between the three of us.

Kai tilts his head to the side, looking at me. "What do you mean?"

"Your eyes," I answer, looking at him in awe. "What does pink mean?"

His face turns the same color as his pink eyes. "Uh, it can mean a lot of things. Passion, lust, love."

Love?

But, no. It's not love. We've only known each other for two days.

But lust?

Maybe.

Is that what I'm feeling now?

I feel like my body is on fire and I have this throbbing need that just won't lessen.

Is that what lust is?

I've never felt lust before in my life. I've only read it described in books. And this... It's so much better than anything I've ever read.

But I also know...

Shifters can smell arousal. There is no hiding it. And my face grows warm with embarrassment as I realize all four of my mates know exactly what I'm feeling right now. Because even though Kai isn't a shifter, he can still feel my emotions because he's fae.

I put my hands to my face, wanting to hide myself.

Why do I have to be so embarrassing?

"It's normal." Levi pulls at my hands, making me look at him. "And even though you can't tell, I'm pretty damn turned on myself."

"It's the mate bond," Kai informs me. "It wants to be completed. It will only get worse with time, until you complete your bond with us."

I didn't know that.

Of course I didn't know that. I haven't been at Shifter Academy to learn these things. The teachers at my pride didn't think teaching me everything was important. And the mate bond they deemed not important. They probably thought that I would never find my mate. That's what everybody in my pride thought.

Poor, ugly Layla.

The runt.

Nobody will ever want her.

Maybe they thought they were doing me a favor by not teaching me.

"I've never felt this before," I admit, chewing on my lip. "It almost hurts. I'm throbbing."

I close my eyes as I realize what I just said out loud.

I take a deep breath before I get the courage to open my eyes, and I find it's not just Kai and Levi looking at me with hungry eyes. Tucker and Mateo are there too.

I want nothing more than to explore these feelings with them.

But if I do...

The mate bond isn't just physical. Completing the mate bond would merge our souls together, and I'm not sure if I'm ready to share what is in my soul with these guys. I'm worried that they won't want me anymore if they see just how badly I am damaged. So for now, this can't happen.

But I so wish it could.

# What's not to like?

Kai holds my hand as we walk to the party.

Mateo and Tucker are both grumpy tonight, and I think it's my fault. I mean, I did get them all hot and bothered, then I didn't let things go any further. Well, they went nowhere at all. That's like the worst kind of torture a shifter can go through after meeting his mate.

Levi and Kai, on the other hand, seem to be doing okay. I mean, I know they wanted me too, that much was clear, but they seem to be more accepting of the fact that I'm not ready yet. Not that Tucker and Mateo *aren't* accepting. I just think it's harder for wolves and bears, considering how possessive they are.

I want to make friends, and coming here to a party will be good for me, even though I'm nervous.

"I hope everybody likes me," I say aloud to Kai, as we follow Tucker and Mateo. Levi is walking behind us.

"What's not to like?" Kai is sweet for saying it.

"I'm a panther. And I see how cruel the panthers are to everybody, not just me. So what if people think I'm like the rest of them?" I want everybody to like me so bad.

I worry my bottom lip between my teeth as we walk closer to the noise.

"You're not like that, Layla. You're so different from the other panthers." He squeezes my hand. "Once they get to know you, they will see."

I hope he's right.

I also hope people will look past the fact that I am a panther and give me a chance to be friendly to them. I really think I could make a good friend to somebody, if given the chance.

The party is a little ways down the beach, the opposite direction of where Mateo was sitting earlier. There is a small bonfire, with chairs all around. There's even a bench that the top is made from a surfboard. It's kind of cool. It reminds me of the town that I used to live in before the alpha council made us move.

A year ago, we were forced to move from our small beach town to a town a difference place about fifty miles away. I'm not sure what happened, but I'm pretty sure our alpha did something bad to the tiger shifters. Since I'm the runt, I wasn't privy to that sort of information, but I miss our old town. The new town we live in isn't close to the water anymore. I mean, there is a lake, but it's not the same as the ocean. Plus, I've seen alligators come and go in the lake. Just because I'm a panther who can heal very easily doesn't mean I want to have to heal from an alligator attack.

"This is so nice." I breathe in the humid air, loving it.

It feels like home.

A lot of people complain about the heat. I mean, the sun has already gone down, and it's still very hot and humid. But I thrive in this weather. Summer makes me happy.

With Kai's hand in mine, I drag him toward the water, wanting to stick my feet in. I take off my flip flops and walk farther down, letting the water wash over my ankles.

I missed the ocean. I missed it so much.

The one thing that always made me happy among the chaos in my pride was going to the beach. I would go at night because humans don't like going there when it's dark. I don't think they can see with their human eyes at night without lights. But I could see just fine. And I could just have fun without worrying about being a bother to anybody else. It was so peaceful and serene.

"I wish I'd worn my bikini under my clothes." I long to go out farther and swim. "I want to go swimming so bad."

"You could always take off your clothes." Levi walks up on the other side of me, smirking.

"I don't think Mateo and Tucker would like that very much." Kai glances backs.

Tucker is talking to some of his pack members, and Mateo is just standing back, his hands in his pockets. He is surveying the party, like he's looking for a threat, then he glances over at me. His eyes soften as he looks at me. I like that about him. That he can be grumpy, yet so sweet to me, even if I am the one who caused his grumpiness.

"They wouldn't mind, if there weren't others around." Levi puts his hands in the front pocket of his jeans. "They are pretty possessive. I am too, I just wouldn't mind showing off Layla's beautiful body to everybody else. She's mine, but they can look and be jealous."

Kai laughs. "I guess tigers are more liberal."

Levi shrugs. "You'd think they would be too. Part of being a shifter is being naked."

He's right about that.

"But I wasn't allowed to run with my pride, so nobody has ever seen me naked before." I don't remember if I told him that.

His mouth drops open. "Damn, I knew you were innocent, but I don't think I realized just how innocent."

My face grows warm at his words.

123

"Just how innocent are we talking?" Kai raises an eyebrow. He knows I'm a virgin, but I'm not sure what else Tucker and Mateo told him.

"Um... I... I've never been kissed. Or hugged. Tucker was the first boy to ever hug me. And holding hands is new. Being touched in any sort of way besides in anger is new." I told Tucker, and Tucker told Mateo, but I haven't told Kai and Levi yet. And judging by how their jaw drops open while they look at me, they had no idea.

"Wait, what do you mean your first *hug*?" Kai asks. "I mean... you have parents."

I shrug. "No mom. Just an alcoholic dad who hates me. And you already know my pride hates me."

Everybody hates me.

But even in my dismal thinking, I can see the light. My mates may not be there just yet, but they will be soon. I can tell they think highly of me. It's only a matter of time. I feel more cherished than I ever have before.

I have hope.

Levi doesn't say a word, he just pulls me into his arms, squeezing me against him.

I can almost *feel* how much what I said hurt him, and I feel guilty. Maybe I should've just kept my past hurt to myself. But I know I won't be able to hide it forever. I know once we complete our mate bond, he will know. It's better to ease them all into it.

"I'm scared to complete our mate bond," I admit.

He stiffens pulling away to look at me. "Why?"

"Because once I do, you will all know the truth. All of my truth. I won't be able to hide it anymore. And that scares me. What if..." I pause, dropping my gaze to stare at my feet, which are buried in the sand. "What if when you see how damaged I am, you won't want me anymore?"

"Layla Rosewood, that simply is not possible," Levi proclaims. "If you could see my heart, you would know."

The power of his words hit me, and I look up at him. My heart is pounding hard and fast.

Maybe this is love.

It's then that I know... it doesn't matter what is in my past. My mates will love me regardless. It was silly to think otherwise.

# Unique.

After playing in the water for a bit, I join the party with everybody else.

It's cool to see Tucker with his pack. He seems a little more relaxed here, and he even goofs off with other members. I've never seen this playful side of him before.

I feel eyes on me, so I glance around the party to see who is watching me. My eyes zero in on two female bears.

Angela and Brittany.

They are glaring at me.

I guess I get where they are coming from. They think that I stole their alpha. Maybe one of them was hoping to be

Mateo's mate. But that's not how it works. We don't choose our own mate. Fate chooses for us.

Something about those two rubs me the wrong way, so I walk over to Mateo and grab his hand. It's the boldest thing I think I've done with any of my mates. They're usually the one who initiates touching. But he doesn't act surprised or anything. He just turns to me and grins widely, then he bends down and kisses me on the cheek.

My heart races like it wasn't just a chaste kiss on the cheek.

I glance back over at Angela and Brittany, and the two of them storm off, clearly unhappy about their future alpha showing me any kind of affection.

But those two are forgotten as I step closer to my mate.

I want to give Mateo a hug, but I'm so nervous to do it. I mean, holding hands is one thing. But a hug? It's silly to be nervous over such a thing, but I can't help it.

Mateo looks at me, furrowing his brow. "What's wrong, Layla?"

How did he know?

I sigh, looking toward the ground. "You'll think it's silly."

He puts his hand to my cheek, gently stroking it with his thumb. "Nothing you desire is silly to me, or have you not realized yet that you are my everything?"

Finally, I look at him. "I want a hug."

A broad grin envelops his face. He doesn't respond. He just pulls me into his arms and embraces me.

Hugging Mateo is everything I imagined it would be. He's so much bigger and taller than me. I wouldn't be surprised if he outweighed me more than double or triple. And it's pure muscle. Despite how much my mate eats, he doesn't have an ounce of fat on his bones. And as hard as his body is, he holds on to me so softly.

He eventually pulls back. His lips brush against my forehead.

"I will hug you any time. You don't have to ask." He rests his hand on the small of my back, like he doesn't want to let me go, which is just fine with me.

I lean my head into him. The top of my head doesn't even reach the bottom of his chest.

I wonder if I am the smallest alpha's mate there has ever been, but then I remember the fairy girl. She is definitely smaller than me, but she's a fae. She's *supposed* to be small. I'm a shifter. I should be tall, like the others.

"Hey, Mateo, why do you think I'm so much smaller than all the other shifters?" It's something I've wanted to know my whole life, but it's never been something I've been brave enough to ask. I guess I knew that any answer I would be getting from my dad or my alpha would just be them mocking me. But maybe there is a real reason.

Mateo lifts one shoulder in a shrug. "I don't know. It doesn't matter to me or the others how tall or short you are, that's not important. If anything, Kai and the rest of the fae prove that even if you're small you can still kick ass. He took on all those panther shifters the other day like it was nothing."

That was pretty awesome.

"Maybe your mom was small too," he suggests.

Maybe.

But I have no way of knowing.

I don't know if my mom is even still alive. If she were, certainly she would be with my dad, right?

Mates never separate. I mean, maybe they could, in theory, but why would you want to leave your soulmate? So, she has to be dead.

I've always thought my mom was dead, just because the way my dad is. He drinks so much. Maybe he does it to forget.

"I wish I could ask my dad about her." I have wanted to know *something* my whole life. I'd love to see a picture of her. Did she have strawberry blonde hair too? And what about my grandparents? Are they still alive?

I don't even know my mother's name.

At the mention of my dad, Mateo's eyes flash black, and I know his bear is close to the surface. I want to change the subject, because the last thing I want is for him to shift here. He doesn't have any clothes here, and I don't want other girls seeing my mate naked.

"Maybe you can introduce me to some people." I step back from him a little but grab onto his hand. "I don't really know anybody here besides you and the rest of my mates, and it might be nice to make some friends."

"Why do you need friends? You have us." His hand tightens in mine.

"I don't know." I shrug. "I've never had friends before, so I think it could be fun to have a friend. And I'd hate to try to make friends on my own and end up becoming friends with girls like Angela and Brittany."

I cringe, thinking about how awful they've been to me. I don't think I could ever be friends with somebody like them, but you never know. I'd like to avoid that situation altogether.

He huffs. "Have one of the other guys introduce you. This is Tucker's pack. He knows them. Or maybe Levi or Kai, they're the outgoing ones."

Mateo isn't outgoing?

No, he's the future alpha. He is outgoing. He's got this natural charisma about him that just draws people in.

"You don't know anybody?" I question.

"I do." He pauses, taking a long breath. "I just... I'm the future alpha of the bear shifters, so people try to use me sometimes. I just keep to myself because it's easier."

I hadn't even thought about that... about people using him because of his status.

I move my hand up, touching his forearm. "I'm sorry. That must suck to have people use you like that."

He shrugs. "It is what it is."

I look at him through my lashes. "Mateo, you know that I don't care about any of that, right? You being Alpha doesn't matter." I pause. "Well, it does matter. You're Alpha. It's important. But I wouldn't care if you were an omega."

His eyes widen. "Really?"

I nod, hoping that he didn't think I was really like that.

"I didn't think you were using me, don't think that." He shakes his head. "Just, you saying it wouldn't matter if I were an omega... that means a lot."

I shrug. "If the panther pride had an omega, I'd probably be it."

"It doesn't matter what position you were in your pride, because in my pack, you're an alpha's mate." He grins proudly.

An alpha's mate is equal to an alpha. Though not always matched in strength, the alpha's mate's commands must be obeyed by the pack.

"Will it be weird for the bear alpha's mate to be a panther?" I tilt my head, considering how strange it will be for my tiny panther to be running with giant bears.

He shakes his head. "Nah. Not weird. Unique."

Unique.

I like that.

I guess me and my mates together are just that—a little, or a lot—unique.

## Monday, August 24
# First day.

Today is the day.

The day I officially start Shifter Academy.

Today, I will be going to my classes for the first time, and I will be meeting all my fellow classmates.

Last night, Mateo never introduced me to anybody at the party. I get why he didn't want to. He is worried that since people know I am his mate, they will try to use me to get close to him. But I hope he knows that not everybody is like that. There are some good people out there. Even I, who was raised in a pride of abusive panthers, know that not everybody is evil.

Even in my pride there were a few nice people. The pride doctor, for example, was wonderful. He always took great care of me when I was injured and he never talked down to me. And when my alpha would beat me, a couple of girls not much older than me would always stay behind to check over my injuries and see if I was okay. I could see the kindness in their eyes while they tended to me. They gave me hope that not everybody is a monster.

I think that not all shifters are power hungry like Mateo thinks. And I think that *maybe* it's possible for me to make a friend while I'm here.

In books, girls always have friends. Usually a girlfriend who they can talk about things with. I've always wondered what it would be like to have that. To gossip, chat, and maybe even have sleepovers.

Eh, maybe not sleepovers. Sleepovers would mean I couldn't cuddle with Kai or one of my other mates, and I don't think I'd like that.

Last night, Mateo insisted I sleep in the bed and not on a cot. And I told him I'd only sleep on the bed if he did too. So somehow I ended up in the middle of the big bed with Mateo on one side and Tucker on the other. I woke up with both of them snuggling me this morning, and I'm not upset about it. In fact, I hope to wake up in the arms of my mates every single morning.

I study myself in the mirror, eyeing my school uniform. I still look like me, but somehow not at all like me. I seem... happy. My eyes are brighter, there is actually a smile on my face, and I literally look like I'm glowing.

This is what happiness looks like.

I knew coming to Shifter Academy would change my life, I just didn't know how much.

I don't know why the school forced Alpha George to allow me to come, but I am so glad that they did. He wouldn't have let me come any other way. Then, I never would've met my mates. I push that scary thought away for another time. Right now, I'm just happy that I am here.

As my mates and I sit down in the dining hall for breakfast, Tucker hands me an envelope. "This is your schedule."

I raise an eyebrow. "I thought I already got my schedule."

"Dean Westwood thought it was best to not put you in class with the panthers. Usually we are with our pack or pride, but you are going to be in class with one of us," Tucker explains.

My shoulders sags in relief as I open the envelope.

I had no idea that I was going to be in class with my pride, but I am so glad to know that Tucker made sure I wouldn't be. That would be an actual tragedy.

I scan the schedule.

**9am:** *Mating Rituals*
**10am**: *Supernatural History*
**11am**: *Modern English*
**12pm**: *Lunch*
**1pm**: *Trigonometry*
**2pm**: *Defense*

Trigonometry?

Gross.

"You have defense with me." Mateo sits up, grinning proudly.

I figured.

He said he wanted to be the one to train me, and I'm going to let him be in charge if it makes him feel better.

Levi gets up to skim my paper. "You have mating rituals with me."

He smirks.

Oh, gosh.

Why do I get the feeling that is going to be an awkward class?

"Supernatural history and trig with me." Kai grins. "I get two classes with you."

"That leaves me with English," Tucker says. "Not bad."

And everybody has lunch period together, so I'll get to see them all then.

"It's a shame they don't just blend everybody in the classrooms together." I take a drink of the coffee that Tucker brought me, surprised by how good it is.

"That would cause chaos." Mateo takes a huge bite from his sandwich.

"Why?" I ask, taking a bite from my own.

"Everybody would probably end up fighting," Levi admits. "I mean, it's not like shifters get along with shifters outside of their species."

I take another bite of my food, wondering if this is really going to work. If Levi is right, and shifters don't get along with other species, how long will it be before my mates start fighting? How long until they hate each other? How long before they hate *me*?

"Why are you unhappy?" Kai nudges me with me elbow gently.

I shrug. "I guess I just don't get the point of Shifter Academy. We came here to be united, yet it feels like we're more isolated than ever. And I worry that you guys will end up hating each other, or even hating me. None of you are the same species as I am. And Mateo, don't you have to have an heir to take over as Alpha of the bears? What happens if I can't give birth to a bear shifter?"

Nobody says anything for a minute, as if they're contemplating what I said. And I'm glad they're taking it seriously.

"Fate doesn't make mistakes." Kai sits up straighter. "If fate chose us for you, then fate knows we are perfect for you. It doesn't mean we won't fight, because I'm sure we will, but we are family. We will always work things out."

"Exactly." Levi puts his arm around my back. "What fairy boy said."

Kai chuckles.

I relax a bit against Levi.

Maybe this will work.

I look at Mateo, wondering what he thought about what I said, but he's not looking at me. He's got a far away look in his eye, and I can tell he's worried.

It's important for an alpha to have an heir, and I think he's worried I won't be able to give him one.

My chest aches.

What if he doesn't want me if I can't give him an heir?

# Not my favorite class.

Mating rituals is a glorified sex ed class.

Well, I guess it's a little more complex. I know from human books that sex ed is more about teaching safe sex—how to use a condom, birth control, and all of that. Shifters don't have to worry about things like STDs. Plus, from what I understand, a human condom wouldn't do much to protect from shifter sperm.

It takes a very strong birth control for a shifter not to get pregnant, and even that isn't perfect. It's ninety eight percent effective, but still...

It's scary to think about that right now. I just met my mates. The thought of getting pregnant while in high school is terrifying. I don't want that.

I make a note to go see one of the doctors on campus to get on birth control, because I hadn't even *thought* about that yet.

Levi holds my hand as we sit in class, which comforts me. This class is full of tigers, and to be honest, tigers kind of hate panthers. We had this argument with them a while ago. I'm not sure exactly what happened, but I do know it was my alpha's fault. So I can't even blame them for not liking me.

I turn my attention forward, focusing on the teacher, Ms. Wilson.

"It has been our understanding that shifters can only produce children with their mate, but that's actually not true," Ms. Wilson says, catching my attention.

I didn't know that.

Everybody knows that you can't get pregnant by anybody other than your mate. It's why a lot of shifters have many partners before meeting their mates. There really is no repercussions for it.

"We don't know the exact science yet, but it is possible for a male shifter to get a non-shifter female pregnant," Ms. Wilson explains. "That is all we know right now, but I imagine we will uncover more as time goes on. And that is why, for the time being, mating with a human is forbidden."

Forbidden?

My eyes widen at that.

I didn't know that.

My pride dates humans. I know that. I've seen many humans around pride land, always with a panther shifter, and usually smelling like sex.

The panthers in my pride like to brag. So after having sex with a human, they'll bring the girl around to show her off to the others. The girl will have no idea that everybody knows what happened. It's kind of sad, really. But what could

I do? I'm the runt. If I even attempted to talk to the girl, I'd get slapped.

A boy in the class raises his hand, and Ms. Wilson points at him.

"What is the punishment for having sex with a human?" the boy asks.

Ms. Wilson stares off into the distance, concentrating on something. "Well, since having sexual relationships with a human can result in a pregnancy, it puts all supernaturals at risk. If a child is born with the shifter gene and the child shifts in front of its human mother, that is bad. So, for the time being, the punishment is Supernatural Island, for ten years."

The entire class gasps, me included.

Supernatural Island is a prison, but it's the worst for shifters who are sent there. While you are in prison there, an elemental will take away your ability to shift. Your body and your animal will be screaming to be let out, but no matter how hard you try, you can't shift. It's complete agony.

I wonder if my pride knows the law. Certainly they do, right?

I try to think if I've seen Alpha George with any humans lately, and I know I have. Just last week he had a couple of girls over. They barely looked old enough to be out of high school, which is his normal. Even though he's over two hundred years old, Alpha George is attracted to younger females.

Laws apply to Alphas too. At least the laws that the alpha council enforce. So Alpha George *should* be at Supernatural Island. He should be locked away for ten years.

But who would turn him in?

Not me. If I did, the pride would kill me. You can't turn against your alpha.

I just hope that Alpha George hasn't put us all at risk so he could have sex with humans. I hope the others in the pride haven't put us at risk.

Ms. Wilson starts discussing the mate bond. Everybody in the classroom turns to look at Levi and me, so I sink down in my seat a little bit, trying to hide.

I don't like when everybody stares at me. I know it's silly, but it makes me nervous. In my pride, everybody ignores me, unless I'm getting hit. That is the only time people pay attention. I swear they get off on watching others suffer. So having these tigers look at me does frighten me.

Levi squeezes my hand, and I know that he's trying to comfort me. If these tigers were to attack me, he would try to protect me.

But nobody is going to attack me. They're only looking my way because they are curious. If I were in their position, I'd be curious too.

Eventually, they grow bored and turn their attention back to the teacher, and I can breathe again.

Shifter Academy is way different than I thought it was going to be, that is true, but at least I have my mates by my side. They make me feel invincible.

Ms. Wilson starts talking about what it's like to complete a mate bond. She's very blunt about it too, and my face grows warm as she starts talking about sex.

I know that completing a mate bond is about more than sex. It's about two people coming together and their souls merging. It's beautiful. But... the bond *is* completed with sex, and that is the simple truth. And hearing her talk about it so freely while I'm sitting beside Levi is a little embarrassing, especially when she tells everybody what it was like when she completed her mate bond with her mate.

"Anthony and I completed our mate bond the first night that we met." Ms. Wilson giggles. "We were on the hood of his car in a field of daisies. It was the 1960's, mind you, so we were a little more free when it came to our bodies. It was a beautiful summer evening, and the stars were so bright."

Oh, gosh.

This is awkward.

Judging from how everybody is looking away from Ms. Wilson, I'd guess they feel the same way as I do.

Ms. Wilson clears her throat. "It's natural to not wait. I know that human culture sometimes creeps its way into our shifter world, but you don't have to wait. Don't fight against your body's urges."

Oh, my gosh.

I close my eyes, wishing I could climb under my desk and hide.

Everybody knows that I haven't completed my mate bond with my mates. When I do complete it, everybody will know because I will smell different. I will smell like my mates. And I know she's not talking directly to Levi and me, but it kind of feels like it.

When the bell rings, I let out a sigh of relief.

Mating rituals... not my favorite class.

# Daisies.

"That was brutal." Levi squeezes my hand as we walk into the hall, heading out of our mating rituals class.

He's not wrong.

That has to be the most embarrassing moment of my life. Maybe even more embarrassing than the time Suzy ripped my shirt off my body and I had to walk home, over half a mile, in just my bra.

Suzy and I wore the same top that day, and she didn't like being caught in the same thing as me. So, she just ripped my shirt off. It was awful. I was only twelve at the time, but I developed early in life.

Even though I am small, really small, I got boobs earlier than any of the other girls in the pride. I didn't like it. But I had to start wearing a bra, and not a training one, when I was eleven. I didn't want anybody else to know that I had to wear a bra. So walking home like that was humiliating.

But today...

Today may have been worse than that.

I hide my face against his shoulder, just wanting the last hour to have never happened.

"I can never show my face in that class again."

Levi chuckles. "Don't worry, Layla. All the others are jealous."

I lift my head and look at him. "Really?"

He nods. "Promise. They wish they had a mate to complete a bond with. And all the guys are jealous because you're sexy as hell, but you're mine, so they don't stand a chance."

I never thought somebody would describe me as sexy.

But Levi makes me feel sexy.

"About what she said, about not waiting to complete the mate bond, I don't want to wa—" I don't get to finish my thought.

"Layla, there you are." Kai grins as he walks toward us.

Levi pulls me into his arms and embraces me. "I'll see you at lunch."

He walks off after our hug, so I turn my attention to Kai.

Kai leans forward and gives me a quick hug.

There has been so much hugging that has happened since I met my mates, and I'm *not* complaining about it. In fact, I like it. A lot.

Once we pull away, he grabs my hand, leading me toward our next class.

"How was mating rituals?" Kai asks.

My face grows warm. "Ms. Wilson is very... liberal with her sex life."

Kai laughs. "Ah, did she tell the story of her and her mate on the hood of his car in the field of daisies?"

"How did you know?" I wonder.

"She tells that same story every year. Usually a few times."

Great. I get to hear that story again. Something to look forward to.

We walk into our next class, which thankfully has *nothing* to do with mating.

History is my favorite subject. I particularly love supernatural history. Hearing about what our ancestors were like and what they had to go through is fascinating to me.

"By the way, the guy who teaches this class is Ms. Wilson's mate," Kai says, as we take our seats close to the back of the classroom.

My head whips around to stare at him. "Seriously?"

He nods.

Great. Now I'll have a face to put on the car with Ms. Wilson in that field of daisies.

Gross.

"This school has weird teachers," I mumble, pulling my tablet out of my bag. I open the app for my Supernatural History book.

This class has fewer students in it, most likely because, aside from me, everybody is fae.

There aren't a lot of fae around. They nearly went extinct a millennium ago. The rest of the supernatural world thought they *were* extinct, so when they came out of hiding it shocked us all.

Since the fae came out of hiding, they have started to find their mates, and they have started to repopulate. But there are only five fae the same age as me, including Kai. So there are only six of us in this classroom.

Even though the story Ms. Wilson told us about completing her mate bond is extremely disturbing, it's also kind of sweet. The faraway look she got in her eyes was a little adorable. I hope I can look back on the day I complete my mate bond with fondness too.

It's then I realize I don't want my first time to be in my dorm room. I want it to be somewhere memorable. Not a field full of daisies, gross. I'll never be able to look at a daisy the same way again. But maybe on the beach, or maybe in that tower that Mateo likes to go to. I just want something that I can look back on with fondness.

Mr. Wilson walks into the room to start class, and I watch him with curiosity. He doesn't appear much older than me. To humans they'd have a hard time believing that Mr. Wilson was alive in the 1960's, but shifters have a very long lifespan. We age slowly. I don't understand the science behind it, or even if it is science. I think it's just magic, plain and simple. Shifters, just like all supernatural beings, are magical. How else could you explain the fact that I am sort of human, but also sort of a panther? I'm both.

Mr. Wilson stops halfway to the front of the room and turns toward Kai and me. He looks at Kai and grins. "Congratulations, Kai."

"Thank you, sir." Kai sits up straighter, puffing out his chest.

I know that Kai is proud of the fact that he's my mate. All of my mates seem to be, but I can't figure out why.

Kai puts his hand on my bare thigh, squeezing it under the desk.

I've never been touched this much in my life, and it's a little overwhelming in the best way possible. My thigh tingles where he touches me.

Mr. Wilson begins class, but mostly he's just going over what we're going to be learning this year. Unlike his mate, he decides to let us chill on the first day, which is perfectly fine with me. Ms. Wilson gave us freaking homework, just a half page essay on birth control, but still.

I cringe, wondering if she assigned that because of me. I am the only mated girl in the class, so nobody else really needs to worry about it.

My face grows warm as I realize that's *exactly* why she assigned that.

Oh, gosh.

That's mortifying.

Kai's hand squeezes my thigh again. He's probably wondering why I'm blushing, so I grin at him, pushing my embarrassing thoughts aside.

After Mr. Wilson goes over our schedule, he just lets us hang out for the rest of class, which is pretty cool.

When I went to school at home, I would end up doing all my work at once, and it would take about three hours to get it all completed, then I'd be free the rest of the day. It's a little disappointing that regular school isn't like that too. We actually have to sit there for the entire time, even if we don't need all that time to learn.

"What is making you blush?" Kai turns to me.

Everybody else is having their own conversations around us, so they're not paying attention to us.

Plus, I don't think fae have good hearing like shifters do.

"Uh..." I clear my throat. "Ms. Wilson gave us homework already. We have to write a report about birth control. And now that I think about it, I realize the assignment is just for me, because nobody else is mated."

Kai laughs. "Oh. That's funny."

"It's embarrassing. I bet everyone knows she did it for me." I frown.

He shrugs. "Everybody else is probably jealous. They all wish they could meet their mate. And sex is natural, Layla. There isn't anything to be embarrassed about."

I know he's right. Hearing the words out loud helps me feel slightly better.

"I am curious about sex. I've heard that it hurts the first time." I put my tablet into my bag, and turn toward Kai. "I've heard girls in my pride talk about it before. I'm a little scared about it hurting."

Kai lowers his chin, looking down. "Um... I... Don't know. I told you about my experience with girls, and it's not a lot."

The two girls he was with over the summer.

I wonder if they're girls we go to school with, but I am *not* going to ask. Maybe in this case, ignorance is bliss.

"But I'm your mate, Layla. Me and the others... we would never hurt you. We'll be gentle when the time comes," he promises.

That does make me feel better about everything.

One more thing has been kind of bothering me too, so I decide to ask Kai.

"How do I choose who goes first? And do I have to complete it with all four of you in the same night? That seems like a lot." Especially if it's going to hurt, even a little bit.

Kai grins, shaking his head. "No. You don't have to complete your bond with everybody the same night. As far as choosing, just follow your heart. When the time is right, you will know. I promise not to be jealous if you choose one of the other guys first, because I know that at some point it will be my turn. I have forever with you, and I'm a patient man."

Relief washes over me at his words.

I'm glad it's not a big deal who I choose first, because the thought of choosing was a little taunting.

I'm glad I asked Kai.

# Opening up.

Kai walks me from our history class to my English class, where I meet up with Tucker.

I've spent the most time alone with Tucker, just because I met him first, but I still feel like I hardly know him. He's a quiet guy, which I like about him, but I also want to get to know him more.

Before Kai leaves me alone with Tucker, he gives me a hug. My heart stammers at the contact, and I wonder if this is going to be a thing—them hugging me every time I go to a new class. I really hope so, because I like it.

"Bye, Layla." Kai turns and walks off, leaving me with Tucker.

I turn to him, having to look up.

Kai is my height, so he makes me feel normal about my size. And I'm taller than all of the other fae in our history class, so I almost forgot about the fact that I'm a runt.

Without saying a word, Tucker pulls me against his chest, wrapping his arms around me.

For the first time in my life, I'm not sad about my height. Instead, I find myself liking the way I fit against his body. I like that my head meets his chest. It feels good.

When we pull back, Tucker grabs my hand and tugs me into the classroom. It's already half full, but there are a couple desks toward the back of the room that we take a seat at.

This class is full of wolf shifters, which makes me a little nervous. I know that Tucker will protect me, but panthers do not have a good history with wolves. Come to think of it, we don't have a good history with *any* of the other shifters. But wolf shifters especially.

I've been taught my whole life that wolves are bad, and that they want to destroy all panthers. Of course, I know now that it's not true, but it doesn't stop the fear that I feel around a room full of them.

As if he senses my anxiety, Tucker reaches over and grabs my hand, squeezing it. All the fear and anxiety leaves my body, and I'm able to breathe.

Everything will be okay.

The wolves *don't* want to hurt me.

And... the best part of it all... I am falling for a wolf shifter, and he has done nothing but go out of his way to protect me.

I think about how I smelled him in my town while I was walking to the bus. And he knew I was terrified of him, so he stayed back, and he just watched to make sure I was okay. He spent fifteen hours following a bus just so he could make sure that I was safe. And he waited until he knew that I needed him before approaching. Then he helped me make it safely to the boat. He is everything that a girl could dream of when thinking about her future mate. He's everything *I've* ever dreamed of. And he is mine.

Our teacher is a little late to class, but nobody seems too concerned by it. Everybody is just hanging out, talking to one another. I spot a group of girls toward the front, laughing about something. I feel a little envious of the friendship the girls have. And I wonder if I will ever have friends like that.

"You okay?" Tucker squeezes my hand.

I nod. "Yeah, I think so."

"How are your classes so far today?"

"My first period class was mating rituals. With Ms. Wilson."

He laughs. "Ah, you heard the story about the daisies."

My face grows warm. "Yeah. And then she gave us homework."

"Homework on the first day?" He raises an eyebrow.

"We have to write a paper on birth control." I shake my head. "I didn't realize until after the class that she assigned it because of *me*. The five of us are the only mated pairs in the school right now."

The smile slips from his face. "She seriously did that?"

"I'm sure it's from a good place."

I'm only eighteen, and I'm not ready for the responsibilities of being a mother. And the truth is, I hadn't thought of birth control that much until we got to that class, so maybe it wasn't a bad thing. It's just... embarrassing, because I'm sure everybody knows she only assigned that paper because of *me*.

Tucker's jaw is clenched, and I can tell he's upset on my behalf.

"Hey, it's okay," I tell him. "Even though it's embarrassing, it's kind of helpful. My pride didn't teach me a lot about birth control, and I'm not ready for a baby."

Slowly his face relaxes. "I didn't know that. I still don't think she should've made the assignment public. She could've pulled you aside and talked to you."

I cringe at the thought. "Honestly, that would've made me more uncomfortable."

I'm not sure if he believes me, but at least he's not angry anymore. "Do you eventually want kids?"

I nod. "Maybe in like thirty years. Or fifty."

Or maybe even longer.

Shifters don't have a limit on when they can have children. I mean, sure, we do get old. But it'll be a very long time before I'm too old to have children. I want to enjoy time with my mates before then. Maybe we can even travel.

"This is the first time I have ever traveled outside of Florida and away from my pride. And while I adore Florida, I want to know what the rest of the world is like. What do the oceans in California look like? And Australia? What is it like at the Grand Canyon? And I'd love to go to Japan. I want to see the pyramids in Egypt. And I want to stay in one of those huts on the water in Bora Bora. I want to sail the seas around Santorini." I don't typically share my thoughts aloud, but I think Tucker deserves to know what I want.

He moves closer to me, his lips parted. "Layla, that all sounds incredible. I want to do it all with you."

"Really?" My eyes widen. "I figured you would think it was silly."

He shakes his head. "It's not silly at all."

The fact that he says that just further solidifies the fact that he is perfect.

The teacher walks into the classroom. She's carrying a large cup of coffee in her hand, and she doesn't seem in any hurry to get to the front of the class to begin. I get the feeling that she's going to be late to class a lot, and that is completely fine with me.

Tucker doesn't let go of my hand during class.

I'm so glad that I opened up to him. I've been so scared to tell all of them how I feel, because nobody has ever cared before.

Maybe...

Maybe we really can complete our mate bond.

If I share what is in my heart already, then there will be nothing to hide.

I just hope they don't try to kill anybody from my old pride when they see what all they've done to me.

# Defense.

The rest of the day flies by, and before I know it, I'm in my last class of the day.

Defense.

I think it's basically a glorified PE class. We get to learn some fighting skills, and I think sometimes they let us shift and go running. Considering I am the only panther in a class full of bears, I'm not sure if it would be safe to go running with them.

I push my prejudice thoughts away. It's silly to still be scared, but after being taught to fear, it's a hard habit to break.

Mateo holds my hand as we walk into the gym. His hand basically envelops mine, reminding me just how small I am... or how big he is.

All the bear shifters are big, even the females. They are less muscular than the guys, but they are so tall. I'm pretty sure the shortest female bear shifter is at least a foot taller than me.

How can Mateo be attracted to me? I look nothing like the girls in his pack. They belong on a freaking runway. They're stunning. Even Brittany and Angela, who hate me, are beautiful.

I glance from the others in class to Mateo, but he's focused right on me. He doesn't even seem to notice anybody else, and my heart feels as though it's going to burst with happiness.

He's staring at me with a huge grin on his face, like he's proud that I'm here beside him. He scoots closer to me.

I look up as a younger girl bounces toward us. She has her long blonde hair tied into a ponytail, and her brown eyes are wide.

"Mateo, when are you going to introduce me to your mate?" The young girl pouts.

She can't be more than fourteen, but already she's so much taller than me. She's a beautiful young girl. I guess she's a member of Mateo's pack.

Mateo rolls his eyes. "I don't want to scare my mate away before I've had a chance to woo her."

The girl laughs. "If you haven't managed to woo her by now it seems like you might be the one who is going to scare her away, not me."

Mateo glances from the girl to me. "Layla, this is my *very* annoying younger sister, Zoey. Zoey, this is my mate, Layla. And watch what you say to her, because someday I will be your alpha."

Zoey rolls her eyes but grins. "Layla, hi. It's nice to meet you. You are so pretty." She grabs a piece of my hair. "I've never seen a panther with your color of hair. Is this your natural color?"

I stare at her with wide eyes, and I nod. "Yeah, it's my natural color."

I don't know what to make of Zoey. She's very... friendly. And not afraid to touch people, which makes me feel a little uncomfortable, but this is Mateo's little sister, so I know she won't hurt me or anything.

"Forgive Zoey, she hasn't learned personal boundaries yet, apparently." Mateo smacks her hand away from me.

She grins. "Sorry. I come from a big family. We like to touch and hug and stuff."

That kind of doesn't surprise me. Mateo is very touchy feely. He likes to hold my hand and touch me, so it makes sense that his family is like that.

"How big is your family?" I ask, turning to Mateo.

Zoey answers for him. "Mateo is the oldest, obvi. But then there is me. I'm fourteen. We have two twin brothers who are thirteen. And I have no idea what my parents were thinking, but I have another set of twin brothers who are twelve. Another sister who is nine. A brother who is seven. And our mother is pregnant again. With twins again this time."

Oh, wow.

That's a lot of babies.

A lot of *twins*.

Like, yikes.

Zoey laughs, pointing at me. "The look on your face. Oh, gosh. Mateo, she just realized twins run on your side of the family. She's never going to want to mate with you."

I actually hadn't thought of that. But she's right. The twin gene *does* come from the male side, at least from what I've read in my biology classes.

Mateo moves closer, putting his arm around my shoulder and pulling me close to him, like he's trying to protect me from his little sister. "Zoey, don't you have other things to do? Like drown yourself in the ocean perhaps?"

She narrows her eyes. "Fine. I can tell when I'm not wanted." Zoey looks at me, her face softening. "It was super great to meet you. I don't know what a girl as pretty as you sees in my brother, but welcome to the family."

Zoey turns and walks off, and I'm left standing there to process her words.

She thinks I'm pretty?

Or maybe she said it to be nice.

"Sorry about her."

I shrug, letting him know it's not a big deal. "She was sweet."

He snorts. "Yeah. Sweet is about the last adjective I'd use to describe Zoey."

Of course he'd say that, she's his little sister. I'm sure he finds her annoying.

"I had no idea you had such a big family." I worry my lip between my teeth, wondering if he wants a big family too.

"It's not a big deal." He tightens his arm around me, and we walk forward with the rest of the crowd.

Our defense teacher stands at the front of the class. I'm surprised to see that our teacher is actually a panther. I had no idea that any panther shifters worked for the school. I don't recognize the guy at all. I've never seen him at any of our pride meetings.

The teacher looks up, his eyes locking with mine. His cocks his head, probably wondering *why* I'm here, in a class full of bear shifters. Mateo growls at him, so the teacher lowers his head, looking away.

I glance from the guy to Mateo, my eyebrow raised.

"Mr. Wells has worked at Shifter Academy for hundreds of years," Mateo quietly answers my unasked question. "He's not a member of your pride. His dad was Alpha a long time ago, and when Alpha George killed his dad, he kicked Mr. Wells from the pride."

That's horrible.

But it doesn't surprise me. That absolutely sounds like something Alpha George would do. He wouldn't want any reminders of the pride that once was.

Today, Mr. Wells is taking it easy on everybody, since it's the first day back. He is just making us run five miles in our human forms.

"Running five miles is *easy*?" I ask.

Because even though I'm a shifter, I can't remember the last time I *ran* five miles. I'm more of a... read a book kind of girl. I've never been athletic.

But... if I really want to prove that I'm strong, I have to do this.

"Five miles is very easy." Mateo laughs as we take off on our run.

He paces beside me, even though I know he probably wants to run faster. His legs are twice as long as mine, so my strides are a lot shorter. But he stays beside me, never complaining.

I'm out of breath after the first half mile.

This is hard.

And embarrassing.

I swear the air is getting thinner.

Even though my strides are getting shorter and I am slowing down, Mateo stays by my side the entire time. I notice even Zoey is hanging back with us, running only a little ways ahead.

I have no idea how I do it, but I manage to make it to five miles. Sweat is pouring off of me, and I am breathing so heavy, but I did it.

Mr. Wells asks me to stay behind once class is over, which doesn't surprise me. He's probably going to tell me that I'm too weak to be in his class.

Mateo stays with me, of course, and we approach Mr. Wells.

"Layla Rosewood, right?" Mr. Wells asks.

I nod, wondering how he knows my name. But then again, a panther with four mates? He's probably heard about me.

Mr. Wells pauses to examine me, his eyebrows raised. "I'm really glad that you're finally here."

Finally here?

Why does he say that like he knows I have been waiting for an invitation from Shifter Academy?

He turns his attention to Mateo. "You know you're going to have to spend time training her, right? She's nowhere near as strong as she needs to be."

Mateo's jaw tightens and he nods.

"I hear you are going to do an alpha challenge for her, but even when you win, Alpha George won't let her go easily." Mr. Wells sighs. "You won't kill him either. It would be easier if you did, but your heart is too big for that."

He's not wrong.

I know that Mateo won't kill Alpha George. Once he has him pinned, he will let him go.

"Alpha George hates me. Why won't he just let me go?" I ask.

But I already know the answer.

It's a pride thing.

Mr. Wells smiles at me, but I can tell it's forced. "Layla, you are too sweet for your own good. The two of you, keep your head up." He glances to Mateo. "And you, teach this girl how to fight."

Mateo nods.

When I first came here, Mateo was so against training me. But now... now it looks like Mateo has had a complete change of heart. And not just because of the conversation I had with him.

Maybe...

Maybe now he sees that I really need the help.

I don't want to be weak anymore.

# Alpha Scott.

Later that night, I'm sitting by Kai on the bed. We're doing our trig homework together, but more like he's copying down all my answers.

I shake my head at him. "You're not going to learn anything if you just keep copying my answers."

He smirks. "Actually, I'm hoping once we complete our mate bond you'll share answers with me through our bond."

I gasp, pretending to be shocked.

"No cheating off Layla's tests." Mateo crosses his arms over his chest.

Kai winks at me, then turns to Mateo. "Your alpha voice doesn't work on me. I'm not a shifter. But I seriously was joking."

"Does his alpha voice work on any of us?" Levi sits down on the bed beside me. "I mean, he's not technically our alpha."

"He'll be Layla's alpha soon, when he issues and wins the alpha challenge," Kai points out. "How long is it going to take Alpha George to get here anyway?"

Tucker gets up from the desk where he was sitting and walks toward us. "The longer Alpha George delays, the better. I know the alpha challenge is our only option, but the more it's delayed, the better."

Mateo shrugs. "I don't know, I kind of want to get the whole thing over with. I'm tired of this looming over us."

There is a knock on the door, so Kai jumps up to answer the door.

"I'm worried," I admit.

Like, really worried.

I know that alpha challenges are *to the death*. That is how they are designed. I know Mateo won't be killing Alpha

George, but if Alpha George can win somehow... Mateo doesn't stand a chance. He won't be merciful. But I don't want to say *that* out loud because I don't want Mateo to think I doubt him.

It's complicated.

Kai opens the door and takes a step back. "Alpha Scott."

Alpha?

I look up and see a very large man standing in the doorway. He's about the same height as Mateo, but he's slightly more buff. I smell that he is a bear.

This must be Mateo's dad.

Mateo looks a lot like his father. He has the same dark hair and dark eyes. And now, while he looks angrily at his son on the bed beside me, I can't help but notice he even holds his jaw the same way when he's angry.

"What is this I hear about an alpha challenge?" Alpha Scott enters my room.

I swallow hard, scooting away from him.

He's scary as hell.

"How did you even hear about that? I haven't even challenged him yet." Mateo stands up, not at all seeming frightened of his dad.

"You're not an alpha, son. You can't do an alpha challenge." Alpha Scott's eyes soften as he looks at his son.

"The law says I can. It says a second in command can issue an alpha challenge." He makes direct eye contact with his father, not backing down. He's determined. "I respect you as my alpha and as my father, but there is nothing you can say that can make me back down from this."

Alpha Scott turns his attention to me. "Is she the panther?"

Mateo steps between me and his father, blocking his view from me. "She is my mate. And I *know* you would do the same thing if our roles were reversed."

"Let me do the alpha challenge." His dad's voice isn't as harsh now. I don't know him, but even I can hear that he's frowning. He doesn't want anything to happen to his son.

"You don't know what he's done to her, Dad." Mateo's voice breaks, but he doesn't back down. "If it were mom, you wouldn't let anybody else fight for you. I can't let you fight this for me. I have to do it myself."

I look scoot over, looking around Mateo. Alpha Scott lowers his head, letting out a long sigh. "I can see that you've made up your mind."

Mateo nods. "I have, Dad."

"Okay." He steps back, letting his son have this victory. "Will you at least introduce me to your mate?"

Mateo turns toward me, most likely seeing if it's okay with me.

I jump up from the bed.

I want to meet his dad. I want to meet all of his family, and the family of my other mates too. I just thought I'd meet them when I was a bit more prepared, not after they burst into my dorm room on a random Monday night.

I walk up beside Mateo. "Hello, Alpha. It's nice to meet you. I'm Layla Rosewood."

"Just Scott." Alpha Scott holds out his hand to shake mine. "It's an honor to meet you, Layla. I wish it were under better circumstances."

"It's nice to meet you as well." After he shakes my hand, Mateo grabs onto it, comforting me.

"How did you find out about the alpha challenge? We haven't told anybody," Mateo questions.

The rest of my mates are all just standing, watching this play out. I'm sure they don't want to be disrespectful to Alpha Scott.

"I heard a few rumors. I mean, it doesn't take a genius to figure out that this is what you would do. Everybody knows how cruel the panther alpha is. It's what I would've done." Alpha Scott's eyes are soft, even as his voice is harsh, but I can see the worry in them. He's scared for Mateo.

"Alpha George will cheat," I blurt out. "He will play dirty and he will do whatever it takes to win. This isn't about *me*. This is about his pride. If he loses, he will look weak, and other panthers will want to steal his alpha spot."

"That's what I was afraid of." Alpha Scott focuses his stare on me. "But I don't want you to worry about that. Alpha Frank and I have a few tricks up our sleeve."

"My alpha is here?" Levi steps forward.

Alpha Scott nods. "Yes. But that is all I can say for now. I don't believe the panther alpha will linger much longer. You kids get a good night's sleep. You're going to need it."

I don't like the sound of that.

"Mateo, may I please speak with you outside for a moment?" Alpha Scott asks.

Mateo nods. He squeezes my hand. "I'll be right back."

I watch as Mateo leaves the room with his dad. My heart feels like it's being ripped in half when he exits the room.

Why do I have such a bad feeling about this? About *all* of this.

"Don't worry." Tucker puts his hand on my shoulder. "Alpha Scott knows what he's doing. He won't let anything happen to Mateo."

I hope he's right.

I do know that Alpha Scott was probably right about Alpha George not lingering. Once he hears about all that has gone on since I got to school here, he will be on his way.

# Tuesday, August 25
# **Nobody can stop them.**

Last night, when Mateo went out to talk to Alpha Scott, he didn't come back for a few hours. Everybody was already in bed by the time he returned. I was awake and waiting for him, but he didn't say a word. He just climbed onto his cot and went right to sleep.

I wonder what Alpha Scott said to him. What if his dad doesn't approve of me? I mean, he didn't seem very happy last night, but I think he was mostly focused on the fact that Mateo is going to issue an alpha challenge to Alpha George.

I'm worried about that too.

The alpha challenge.

I try not to think about it, because when I do, I just worry more, but after how his dad reacted... maybe I should be worried.

Mateo, Levi, Tucker, Kai, and I head down for breakfast before class, but now all of my mates are acting weird, and

I'm wondering what is going on. But when I question them, they just tell me that everything is fine. It's frustrating, because I *know* something is going on.

But what?

Is Alpha George on his way now or something? I mean, I figured he'd be coming down soon. There is no way somebody in my pride hasn't contacted him yet. The question is, does he really care enough about a runt like me to come down right away? I figured he'd come soon, but maybe in a few weeks, or even a month.

Or maybe it's something else entirely. Maybe Alpha Scott told Mateo what I've known all along—that he is too good for me. Maybe he believes it. Maybe all my mates do.

I sigh, trying not to be so cynical and self-loathing in my thoughts, but being told all these horrible things about myself my whole life... It's hard not to believe them.

When we get to the dining hall, Mateo turns to me, putting his hands on my shoulders. "Zoey is going to eat breakfast with you. The guys as I have something to do."

I turn to him, confused. "Wait, what?"

But he doesn't explain. The four of them turn and leave the dining hall. That's when I notice Zoey standing there, a tray of food in her hand.

"Mind if I sit here?" She motions to a seat across from me.

I shake my head. "Go ahead."

But I'm still in shock.

What is going on?

"They're acting weird, right?" Zoey takes her seat in front of me. "I mean, my brother is *always* weird, but that was over the top, even for him."

I shrug. "Your dad came last night, and he's been acting weird since then."

Her eyes widen. "My *dad* is at Shifter Academy?"

She didn't know?

I tuck a piece of hair behind my ear. "Uh, yeah. He came to our dorm last night."

She huffs. "Why did nobody tell me? I even talked to my mom this morning."

I don't know how to respond, so I just take a big bite of my food. I'm not hungry, but I know that I need to eat. I have a feeling that it's going to be a long day, and I'm going to need the calories.

When I get about halfway done with my first sandwich I notice a few members of my pride walk in the dining hall. Their eyes hone in on me. They're probably noticing that my mates aren't at breakfast with me.

I send up a silent plea for them not to come over, and I turn my attention back to my food, desperate to not pay any attention to them.

They're not worth it.

I stuff another bite in my mouth.

Zoey smiles. "You know, everybody has noticed how different you are from the others in your pride. Everybody *actually* likes you."

"Really?" That surprises me, because I didn't think anybody liked me. Why would they? I haven't even spoken to anybody, other than my mates.

"Why do you seem so shocked?" She shakes her head. "I haven't gotten to talk to you very much, but I already know you're nice. And you're really pretty."

"I don't look like other shifters, especially bear shifters." I lower my head. "I don't see how Mateo can be attracted to me at all."

"You don't look like other shifters, you're right. But that's *not* a bad thing. Who wants to look just like everybody else? Besides, Mateo has never even been remotely interested in those other girls."

I glance up at her. "Really?"

"Yes, really." She shakes her head, laughing. "Girl, your pride really did a number on you. But I'm serious. I know Angela and Brittany have given you a hard time, but only because they're jealous. Mateo has never been into them."

"But they're beautiful."

"Snooty bitch really isn't his type."

I laugh, because her description of them is spot on.

I'm glad Zoey feels the same way about them as I do, and I'm also glad that Mateo never dated them.

"What about other girls?" I question. "I mean... has Mateo ever dated anybody?"

She shakes her head. "Not that I know of, but that's probably something you should ask him."

She's right.

I need to talk to Tucker and Mateo about their past dating life. I've spoken with Kai and Levi about it, but for some reason, I've been too scared to ask the two of them, especially Mateo.

Because he's the future alpha.

Alphas can get *any* girl they want.

So why would he want me?

"Where are your boyfriends?"

I *know* without looking that the condescending voice belongs to Jack. I also know that Brady will be standing behind him.

Zoey climbs to her feet, crossing her arms over her chest. "They're not her *boyfriends*, they're her mates."

I look over at Jack. He has his eyes narrowed, not even acknowledging Zoey. He's looking at me.

"How did you trick them into thinking they're your mates?" Jack shakes his head. "Alpha is going to be so disappointed. He told you not to embarrass the pride, yet here you are doing just that."

How does Jack know what Alpha told me? I haven't told *anybody* about that.

"Alpha told us that if you take a step out of line that we can punish you how we see fit," Jack continues. "And seeing as your bodyguards aren't here, we have to follow Alpha's orders."

My heart races in fear, because I know I won't be able to do a thing to stop them. Behind Jack, Brady is standing there, along with eight other members of my pride. And they're strong—a lot stronger than I am.

Brady swings the first punch, hitting me right on my nose. His hit is so hard that my vision darkens and I see stars. I start to fall over, but I steady myself at the last second, stumbling back. But before I have a chance to recover, another punch is swung, this time at my stomach. It's not as hard of a punch as the first one, but it still hurts.

I hear Zoey yelling, and I look up and see her trying to fight. I open my mouth to tell her to stop, I don't want her to get hurt because of me, but another punch is swung at my face again. This time, I go down.

That doesn't deter them whatsoever. I start feeling kicks at my side. I whimper, but I don't scream. I won't give them the satisfaction of knowing that what they're doing hurts. If they knew how much it hurt, they would enjoy it so much more.

I curl into a ball, covering my face with my arms. I've learned through many beatings that if I curl up I won't hurt as bad once this is over. I can recover fast.

Even though I don't want my pride to know how much they're hurting me, I can't help the tears that escape. I thought this was over. I thought I was done getting beat by them. I thought... well, it doesn't matter what I thought, because I know now that I will never get away from my pride.

I can't stop them.

My mates can't stop them.

Nobody can stop them.

I can hear Zoey screaming at them to stop, and even through the pain of my pride kicking me and hitting me, it feels good to know that I have somebody on my side. I have my mates. And I have Zoey. I'm not alone anymore, and *nobody*, not even my pride, can take that away from me.

One blow lands on my lower back, and I can't help but scream at the pain.

I know that they broke my spine. It's not the first time they've done it, and I'm certain it won't be the last. But no matter how many times it happens, I never get used to the pain.

The kicking stops once I start screaming. And I have no idea *why* they stopped, but it doesn't matter. My vision starts to go black again, this time because of the pain. I welcome the darkness with open arms.

# Taken care of.

When I open my eyes again, I am lying on the bed in my dorm room. I know it's my bed because it's so soft and so warm. I can smell my mates—all four of them.

I try to sit up a little, but the pain in my back reminds me that it's broken. I know it will heal, it's already started, but broken bones take a little longer to heal completely.

Still, I cry out because of the pain, unable to stop myself.

When my mates hear me call out, they all run over to the bed to check on me, now realizing that I am awake.

"I'm okay." I say the words before they can ask how I am. I don't want them to worry about me.

"Your spine is broken. I don't think *okay* is a word I would use." Kai sits on the bed beside me.

"What happened?" I ask.

"Your pride beat the crap out of you." Levi sits beside Kai. "Do you not remember?"

"I remember that part." Though I wish I didn't. "What happened *after* that?"

"We could feel your distress through our mate bond and we came running back to you." Kai reaches his hand up and gently strokes my face. "We didn't get back soon enough."

"We shouldn't have left in the first place." Tucker's voice is strained. Even though I can't see his face, I already know that he's on the verge of his wolf coming out. He is pissed.

"Why did you leave?" I was curious why they left me alone with Zoey in the first place.

"Alpha Scott asked to speak with us." Levi puts his hand on my arm, and I get the feeling that he just needs to touch me, which is fine with me. "We couldn't say no, even though maybe we should have."

"The panthers don't usually eat breakfast that early. Had we known..." Kai's voice trails off.

I know they never would've left me alone if they'd known that there was a chance of the panthers doing this.

"I'm fine." I hope they believe me this time. "What happened is normal for me. It's not the first broken back I've had, and I'm sure it won't be the last. It'll be sore for a few days, but I'll be good as new soon."

Mateo has remained quiet up until this point, but he steps forward now. His eyes are as black as the midnight sky. "You're *not* fine, Layla. Nothing about what happened to you is fine. It's completely fucked up."

I reach toward him, trying to touch him, but when I lift my arm I have an intense pain in my shoulder that makes me cry out again. I let my arm fall back to the bed.

"Your shoulder popped out of socket too. I put it back in for you, so it'll heal faster." Levi's eyes are full of tears as he says it.

It's then that I realize just how hurt my mates are over this.

Yes, I am used to this. And yes, they know about the abuse I've suffered. But this is the first time they're really seeing it with their own eyes. I know that if our situations were reversed, I would be a complete mess. I would hate to see them hurt, just as I'm sure they hate seeing me hurt.

"What happened after I blacked out?" I ask.

"We took care of them," Tucker growls.

"Zoey and I got you to the doctor on campus," Levi explains. "Tucker, Mateo, and Kai took care of the ones who attacked you."

My eyes widen. "Took care of how?"

But nobody answers the question.

And then I know.

"Did you... *kill*... them?" I whisper the words that I'm too scared to say out loud.

"They punched you and kicked you. They literally broke your back. And you're asking if we killed them?" Mateo's voice is low, and his face is red with anger.

I don't know what to say, because I am asking that.

"Yes, Layla. We did. It was our right to protect our mate." Kai's voice is soft as he strokes my cheek.

As much as I don't want to cry, I can't help the tears that escape.

I'm not sure if I'm crying because some of my pride members are dead, or if it's because I never have to go through what I did ever again.

"You cry for them, even after what they did to you?" I can hear the shock in Tucker's voice.

All of my mates are looking at me in disbelief.

"Nobody has ever cared for me as much as the four of you." I try to wipe the tears off my cheek, but I can't lift my arm to do so.

Kai wipes at my tears for me. "I would do it all over again, Layla. I'd do anything for you."

"We all would." Mateo steps forward. "I wish I could bring them back just so I could kill them again, slower this time. Death was too easy for them."

"Thank you." I make eye contact with each of my mates. "But you know this isn't the end. Alpha George... He's not going to stand by idly. I'm still a member of his pride."

"Not for long." Tucker leans over and kisses me on my forehead. It's more gentle than I ever thought a wolf shifter could be. "Get some sleep, Layla. You need it."

Even though I didn't think sleep would be possible, my eyes are heavy. I find myself shutting them.

I know my body will heal faster if I can sleep, so I let the darkness envelope me. But before I go completely under, I swear I hear somebody whisper, "I love you."

# Wednesday, August 26
## For me.

I don't wake up again until Wednesday morning.

I literally slept all day long yesterday, and I know my body needed it.

I wake up feeling completely refreshed and energized. My back is a little sore, and I have a few lingering bruises, but other than that, I feel great. Amazing, even.

I've never healed this fast before. But then again, I usually can't just sleep away my injuries. I'm typically too scared to sleep. I always worry that my pride will come and finish the job if I sleep. But yesterday, I was truly safe.

I know there will be repercussions for what happened, but for the time being I am going to rejoice. I am *free* of the members of my pride who have abused me the most. And for the remainder of my time at Shifter Academy, I'm safe.

At least until Alpha George shows up.

My eye has a purple and green colored bruise around it. The bruise will most likely be gone by tomorrow, but it still looks pretty bad. There is also a light bruise on my cheek, but my nose looks fine—maybe a little swollen, but it's barely noticeable.

I sigh, stepping back from the mirror.

"You're beautiful." Tucker kisses the bruise on my cheek softly.

My face grows warm at his compliment.

"Are you sure you want to go back to school today?" Levi shakes his head. "I personally think you should milk the hell out of this. Take another day off. We can stay in bed all day." He winks at me. "Now *that* has potential."

I giggle. "Levi!"

He shrugs. "Can't blame a guy for trying."

Staying in bed with my mates all day does sound like fun, but I also know that I shouldn't hide out in my room. I should face it now.

I'm sure everybody knows what happened. Shifter Academy is a small school. And the fact that the panthers are now missing a tenth of the pride members *is* going to be noticeable. There weren't that many people in the dining hall that early, but the ones who were there are going to talk. There is no hiding what happened.

"Are you guys really not in trouble?" I ask, just to be certain.

I know the laws. And I know that it is legal to kill to defend your mate. It's just... I've never seen anybody actually do it before.

"No. We're not in trouble." Levi bends down and kisses me on top of my head. "Let's go get some breakfast. You're going to need a lot of calories today. You burned a lot yesterday."

When we heal, our body does burn a lot of calories. That might be why I healed a lot faster this time than the times before too. I actually *had* fuel in my body. Maybe my mates forcing me to eat more isn't a bad thing.

Mateo, who hasn't said a word to me yet this morning, walks over and wraps his arms around me. "Everything is going to be fine, Layla. You'll see."

I needed this hug, and I didn't realize just how bad until his arms were tightened around me. I melt into his embrace, loving the way his strong arms wrap around my waist.

Together, the four of us head toward the dining hall. Mateo walks in front, like he's trying to block anybody from even *looking* at me. Kai and Tucker hold my hands on either side. And Levi follows quietly behind us. So quietly that I glance back to confirm he's still there. When he sees me looking, he winks at me.

Levi is sweet. All of my mates are. But Levi does these things when I'm upset to make me laugh. He'll joke about something, or he'll wink at me, just little things like that. And it makes me forget what I was upset about to begin with.

I guess all of my mates have their own things that they do to cheer me up. I don't know what I would do without them. Yesterday would've been a lot worse if they hadn't intervened. Maybe my pride really would've killed me this time. They've certainly threatened to do it enough times.

I have known my whole life that someday my pride is going to kill me. And they've beaten me so bad a few times, I prayed for death. But I'm glad my pleas were ignored, because then I wouldn't be here now. I wouldn't know what true happiness feels like.

When we get into the dining hall, I am too scared to raise my head. I know that everybody is probably staring at me. Kai tugs on my hand, pulling me over to our table, and the rest of the guys go into the kitchen to grab some food.

I take a deep breath, telling myself not to be a chicken. I finally look up, and I'm shocked that nobody is staring at me. People do glance my way ever so often, but nobody is downright staring like I thought they would.

"Mateo said if anybody stared at you or made you feel uncomfortable, he would beat the crap out of them." Kai smirks. "We told everybody what happened. Dean Westwood called an assembly and Mateo addressed the entire school. He gave them a rundown of what happened, because he didn't want everybody gossiping about it, and then he told them about the staring thing."

My jaw drops open.

Mateo did that for *me*?

My heart is so happy, I feel as though it could burst.

"His dad stood behind him too," Kai says. "I know that you think Alpha Scott doesn't like you for whatever reason, but that's not true."

"How do you know that?" My eyes widen as I study him.

He shrugs. "I'm a fae. I can feel everything that you feel. It wasn't hard to guess your thoughts from what you were feeling."

Huh.

"It must be strange to feel what everybody else is feeling. How do you sort out your own feelings from everybody else's?" I focus on him, genuinely curious. I've always wondered about the fae. They're so... mysterious.

"It's different." He shrugs. "I guess I can't explain it any more than you can explain the magic behind shifting."

I suppose I understand. I mean, if he asked me *how* I turn into a panther, I wouldn't know how to answer. Me shifting is literally as easy as breathing. My panther is a part of me, just as Kai's magic is a part of him.

"Do you know how I feel?" I ask.

He laughs. "Layla, I'm not even sure *you* know how you feel."

Fair enough.

"But I do know you feel a lot of confusion. You're angry, hurt, happy, sad, elated, lonely, overwhelmed, and a world of other emotions that you cycle through. It's crazy how fast your mood changes."

He's right about that.

"I also know that you've been on the happy and elated side of things when your mates are around." He puts his hand on my arm. "Layla, we're not going anywhere. You don't have to be scared about us leaving you."

He already knows me so completely.

Tucker, Mateo, and Levi sit down at the table with us. Mateo places a tray in front of me with four breakfast sandwiches on it.

I raise an eyebrow.

He shrugs. "What? I thought maybe you'd be hungry."

I shake my head.

I don't think Mateo will ever stop trying to get me to eat more, but I can't even be mad about it. I know he's doing it because he cares about me. And that is all I've ever wanted in life—for somebody to care about me.

I know I won't be able to eat four breakfast sandwiches, but I will try to eat two whole ones. For Mateo. For all my mates. And even for me.

# That's what scares me.

Later that night after my classes are over, the guys and I study in the main common room. I didn't want to, but they insisted.

I've been telling them that I want to make friends, and now they've decided to take what I've said to heart. But I'd

181

much rather hide in my dorm room after what happened. I want to stay hidden away.

As I am finishing up the last of my homework, I feel eyes on me. I look up from my trig book and see a few people from my pride are staring. I'm not surprised by this. I knew it would take a lot more than Mateo threatening them to get them to stop.

I can see just how angry they are. They're *glaring* at me.

I shiver at their stare.

If looks could kill, I would be dead. And I realize... That's what they want. They want me dead. And if they ever get their hands on me, I will be a goner. I know that.

I hear Mateo growl. The ones staring turn and leave the common room.

"Thanks," I say to Mateo, turning back to my book to finish up my last homework question.

I hate trig.

But I'm surprisingly good at it.

I write out my answer for the last question and I slam my book shut. "Done."

"Good, we can play now." Levi smirks.

"Levi, finish your homework," Mateo growls.

Levi rolls his eyes playfully but looks back at his own book.

"You're not allowed to Alpha everybody," I muse.

Mateo shrugs. "I can try. Besides, I'm bigger."

Kai holds up his hand, a white ball of light sitting on top. "What is that about being bigger?"

I laugh, loving their playfulness.

"Hey, no beating each other up." I point a finger at both of them.

They both lower their heads.

Levi laughs. "Layla is the alpha of the four of us."

Can you imagine? Me, the runt of the pride, being an alpha. It's actually laughable because it's so absurd.

"Speaking of Layla being alpha, I'm going to start your training this weekend," Mateo informs me.

I sit up straighter, my eyes widening. "You mean it? You'll train me to fight?"

He nods. "I told you I would. And now I see that it's important for you to know how to fight."

"Not that we will *ever* leave you alone again," Tucker says.

I am definitely okay with them never leaving me alone again.

My mates aren't stupid. I think we all know what will happen if the panthers ever find me alone.

They won't be merciful. And they won't delay it. They will kill me.

"Alpha George will be coming soon, won't he?" I play with the hem on my skirt. "I mean... it was inevitable that he would come, but he's probably coming sooner now, right? I mean, you killed ten guys in the pride. He'll want revenge."

Nobody says anything.

I finally look up, meeting Mateo's gaze.

"Yes, Layla. I don't think the panther alpha will delay his trip here much longer." Mateo reaches over, grabbing my hand. "But I don't want you to worry. It's my job as your mate to take care of you, and I will take care of your alpha."

Before yesterday, I knew he wouldn't be killing my alpha. But now... now he's mad. He's seen what my pride is capable of and exactly what they have put me through. I don't think he will hold back in the fight. It will be a fight to the death. I just worry what that means for Mateo. Will he be okay? Will he survive this fight? What if Alpha George is able to get the upper hand?

I spot Zoey entering the room. She sees me and walks over.

I wasn't allowed to go to my defense class today. I guess the doctor didn't want me going there until my body had a chance to heal a little bit more. So I haven't seen Zoey since yesterday morning.

"Hey, how are you?" Zoey's eyes scan over my body. "You look a lot better than you did yesterday. I would've come to your room, but Mateo said you were sleeping and he wouldn't let me."

She crosses her arms over her chest as she glares at her brother. I can tell she's upset that he wouldn't let her come.

"Mateo's right, I was asleep. I guess my body needed the rest." I offer her a smile, trying to show her that I'm fine. "I'm all better now."

"Good." Her body relaxes a little at my words. "I'm so sorry about what happened. I tried to protect you, but there were so many of them. A couple panthers held me back from you. It was... awful what they did."

I shrug. "It's not a big deal. My pride... They're always like that. It's not the first beating I've taken. I'm strong."

Her mouth falls open. "Oh, gosh. I'm sorry, Layla. I see now why the guys... I mean..."

Why they killed the panthers that attacked me.

Yeah.

I completely understand why my mates acted the way they did. I know that the panthers who attacked me deserved it, but it's still a lot to take in.

My mates took a life for me. They took several lives for me. And it's something that I can never repay.

"Everything will work out." Zoey puts her hand on my shoulder to comfort me. She must be able to read the distress on my face. "You don't have to worry. Your mates won't let anything bad happen to you. Certainly they've proved that now."

Yeah, they *have* proved that. And I think that is what scares me the most.

I don't want them getting hurt because of me.

# Can't sleep.

I can't sleep.

Even with Mateo and Levi lying beside me.

This bed is too comfortable. The guys are too warm. And I just can't close my eyes.

Every time I do, I see them—Brady, Jack, and the other members of my pride. I see the evil in their eyes as they kick me and punch me. Even though they are gone now, they still haunt my dreams.

I sit up slowly, looking over at the cots. Kai is fast asleep. But when I turn my gaze on Tucker, I see that he is looking at me. He raises an eyebrow in question, probably wondering why I am awake.

As carefully as I can, I climb off the bed. I'm good at sneaking, so I know I don't have to worry about waking them. I tiptoe my way to Tucker's cot.

There is barely room on the cot for him, but he still scoots over, making room for me. I feel a little bad about taking up what little space he has, but I just need somebody to talk to right now.

"You should be sleeping," he whispers, careful not to wake the others.

"I can't." I wish that I could.

"Are you hurting?" His eyes scan my body, as if he's making sure none of my injuries are acting up.

He's sweet.

Nobody has ever cared for me like this before.

"I'm fully healed." I twist my back to prove it to him. "It's not even sore."

"Good." He sighs. "But why can't you sleep?"

I chew on my lip, trying to think of what to say. But I don't want to hide the truth from him. Not anymore. "Every time I close my eyes, I see *them*. They're hitting me and kicking me. And I know they're gone. I know they can't hurt me anymore. But it's like they're still haunting my dreams."

He doesn't say a word, he just pulls me into his arms, squeezing me against him. It's exactly what I needed, and I'm glad that I told him the truth. I needed this.

"I'm not going to let anything happen to you." He promises.

I know it's a promise that he might not be able to keep, but I also know that Tucker will do everything in his power to make sure that he keeps the promise.

"Thank you for keeping an eye on me." I peer up at him when we pull back. "I never told you that, but I appreciate it."

"I shouldn't have let you take the bus." He shakes his head. "I could kick myself for forcing you to spend fifteen hours on that thing."

I grab onto his hand. "It was fine. The bus wasn't that bad. And you were right. If you would've picked me up in my town, I would've been scared of you. The way that things happened was perfect."

"I don't deserve you. How do you always know what to say to make me feel better?" His jaw goes slack, and I know I've stunned him.

"You're the one who always makes *me* feel better." Can't he see that? "I know that I'm not good at this whole mate

187

thing. And I'm so sorry. You deserve so much better than me."

"What are you talking about? How are you bad at being my mate?"

I look at him through my lashes. "Because most mates complete their bond right away. And I haven't even kissed you. None of you."

He grins, understanding on his face. "Layla, I would wait forever for a kiss from you. When the time is right, it will happen. Until then, I will be patient. What kind of mate would I be if I rushed you?"

He says it like it's so simple.

And maybe it is.

But I still wish I were brave enough to lean forward and kiss him.

He puts his hand on my cheek, his thumb gently touching my lips. "I adore you, Layla Rosewood."

My heart swells.

At his words, I lean forward. By the way his eyes widen, I think I've shocked the hell out of him by doing so, and I gently press my lips against his. It's a soft kiss, just a peck. I have no idea what I'm doing, but it doesn't matter. Once I make that first move, Tucker takes over and he kisses me hard. He pulls me tight against him and he devours my lips.

This kiss is so much better than what I've read in books. There are butterflies in my stomach, and my heart is racing. And the best part is, he's mine. This kiss is just the first of many that I will share with Tucker.

In that moment I realize that what I feel for him, what I feel for all of them, is stronger than anything I've ever felt before. And maybe it's too soon to be in love, but it's definitely something strong.

There is something else, though. Besides the feeling of falling for this man, for all these men, my body feels as though it is on fire. And I want more of Tucker. I want...

I want to complete our mate bond, I realize. I want that more than anything.

"Tucker," I whimper against his lips, needing more.

"We have to stop or else I won't want to. I already don't want to." Tucker pulls back, looking at me.

"We don't have to stop."

He pushes a piece of hair behind my ear. "Sweet, Layla, I would love for us to complete our mate bond tonight, but I'm pretty sure Mateo would kill me if I did. After everything that's happened... he would think I took advantage of you."

I roll my eyes. "I will talk to Mateo and tell him it was my idea."

Tucker chuckles, pulling me against him. He kisses me again, but this time it's not as intense. I can tell he's holding back.

I know it's sweet that he's not pushing me to complete the mate bond. I know he's doing it because of everything that has happened. But I kind of wish he'd stop being sweet and just ravage my body.

Since Tucker seems intent on saving my purity for whatever reason, I just reach my hand down to touch myself. My body is throbbing.

He grabs my hand, stopping me. I'm about to fight him when I feel his hand dip under my panties.

Tucker kisses me again, this time harder as he plays with my clit. I can tell that he wants me just as bad from the bulge pressing against my leg, but he doesn't move to pleasure himself. He just touches me.

I reach my hand down to touch him, but he shakes his head.

"Layla, this is about you. Just let me please you." His voice is rough, and I can see that his wolf is close to the surface.

I know that I shouldn't relish in the fact that I've nearly made him lose control, but it turns me on to know that I have this kind of effect on him.

Between Tucker kissing me, and his finger circling me, I come hard against his hand. I bite my lip to keep from calling out, not wanting to wake the others.

He rests his forehead against mine, just breathing. He is breathing just as hard as I am. He lies there for a second before pushing up.

"Where are you going?" I don't want him to go anywhere right now. I want to stay here with him and cuddle. I want to be close to him.

"I'm going to clean up." He points at the front of his pants. "Getting you off was the hottest thing that has ever happened to me."

Oh.

OH.

My eyes widen, and I nod.

Right. He needs to clean himself up.

He smirks, walking off, so I lie back down and wait for him to come back so we can cuddle.

Tucker was right, though.

That was the hottest thing ever. If just touching was that great, I can't imagine how great it will be to complete our mate bond.

# Thursday, August 27
# I don't like this.

"You smell different." Levi tilts his head to the side as he studies me that morning.

We're about to head to the dining hall for breakfast. Even though we have this inevitable alpha challenge looming over us, life still goes on. We have to continue living.

I shrug. "I don't know why."

But then I realize, maybe it's because of what happened last night. I took a shower, but a scent does linger in the air. My face grows warm at the realization, and I really hope that Levi doesn't figure out what it is.

Tucker jumps up from the couch. "We should go to breakfast."

Levi looks between Tucker and me, then he gives me a slow smile, like he knows exactly what happened last night.

"You didn't complete the mate bond," he muses. "But something *definitely* happened."

I want to hide.

Tucker growls at Levi. "Just drop it."

"Why? This is entertaining." Levi leans back in his chair.

I sigh, knowing he's not going to drop it. "We just kissed, that's all."

Levi raises and eyebrow, like he's calling my bluff.

"It's seriously none of your business." Tucker stands from the couch. "Where is Mateo anyway?"

"He had to meet with his dad about something." Levi shrugs.

The bathroom door opens and Kai walks out. I'm glad Kai is here, because maybe Levi will drop the whole me smelling different thing. It's not like I'm trying to keep anything from my mates, but I also don't want to sit here and talk about it.

Now that it's daytime, I'm a little embarrassed. I mean, I enjoyed it. A lot. And obviously Tucker did too. And there is nothing to be embarrassed about. What we did was completely natural. We're mates.

But I also pretty much begged him to have sex with me. In the moment, it felt right, so I'm not going to linger on feelings of embarrassment. What happened, happened. There is no taking it back now. And I wouldn't even if I could.

"What were you guys talking about? Layla's face is bright red." Kai looks from me to Tucker and Levi.

Levi just keeps the smirk on his face.

"Let's get breakfast." I stand up from the bed, ready to get out of this room.

Tucker is the first one out the door. I guess he is feeling awkward about this conversation too.

This is my life now. I have four mates. Four *guys* are going to always be around me. They're always going to be talking and messing around. It's inevitable that they'll be friends too, Kai and Levi already act like they're BFFs.

I groan.

"What's the matter?" Levi walks up beside me, concern in his eyes.

"I just realized that I'm going to be teased for the rest of my existence," I admit.

He laughs.

"Now I need to know what happened." Kai comes up on the other side of me.

Tucker just keeps walking ahead of us.

"I don't know what happened. That's the point. But Layla and Tucker definitely did *something*." Levi smirks.

"You are literally worse than the girls in my pack." Tucker stops and turns to Levi. "If Layla wants to tell you what happened, she will."

The smile falls from Levi's face, and he lowers his head.

I shouldn't keep this from Levi. And the fact that I've hurt his feelings now makes me feel bad.

"We kissed." Which I already told him, but I hadn't told Kai. "And he touched me because I asked him to. That's it. I didn't want to tell you because I didn't want things to be weird. I was also processing it myself."

"You haven't made things weird." Levi grabs my hand. "Honestly, Layla, we're your mates. All of us. There is no need to be embarrassed about anything. Just... maybe next time I can watch."

Tucker huffs, turning forward and walking again.

I'm glad Levi made the joke though, because it *does* make me feel better about everything.

I glance over at Levi as we walk, and I see him watching me.

Maybe it wasn't a joke.

"How are you all just okay with sharing me?" I ask, shaking my head. "The thought of you with another girl makes me want to claw her eyes out."

It's such a hypocritical thing to think, I know it is. But I'm trying very hard to be honest with my mates, and I want them to know how I feel.

"You're not just mine. You're ours." Levi's answer is simple, but I still don't get it. And maybe I never will. It's a fate thing, that much I know. It's the only thing that can be explained.

When Levi, Kai, Tucker, and I walk into the dining hall, everybody turns to look at us as we enter. I honestly thought everybody was done staring, but I guess not. Then again, maybe they only stopped because Mateo threatened them. He's not with us today, so they feel like they can look.

"Am I missing something?" Kai asks, as we walk into the kitchen.

I shrug. "I don't know."

"It's not like Mateo to miss breakfast," Levi muses as we grab our tray of food from one of the men standing by the grill. "Not even for his alpha."

Mateo does like to eat. A lot.

But if his dad needed him, he would be there.

We walk back out into the dining hall and sit down. People are still looking, but I try to ignore them all.

"It is weird. Does anybody know what Alpha Scott wanted?" I grab my sandwich, taking a bite.

"His dad has been helping him train for the alpha challenge." Tucker shrugs, stuffing a huge bite in his mouth.

I did know that. Well, I didn't know about the *training*, but I did know his dad was helping him. It makes sense though.

"Where are the panthers?" Kai glances over at where the panthers are usually sitting, but they're not there.

Strange.

My eyes widen. "Do you think Alpha George is here?"

Nobody says anything.

Maybe he is.

Is today the day?

An uneasy feeling settles over me.

"I don't like this," I admit.

"Neither do I." Kai reaches over and grabs my hand, squeezing it.

This is terrifying.

# He's going to try.

My worry just intensifies throughout the day as I don't see Mateo. I don't see him between classes, I don't see him at lunch, and now that I'm going to our defense class, he isn't here.

It isn't like him to not be around. Ever since what happened with the panthers, I didn't think he would ever again let me out of his sight. And I don't *think* he would unless there was something wrong.

I spot Zoey standing in a corner by herself. I make my way over to her, hoping that she has some answers.

"Zoey, what's going on?" I ask, not even saying hi. Right now isn't the time for chit chat though. I need to know where Mateo is and if he is okay.

"I don't know." She chews on her nail as she answers. "My mom called me earlier. She hasn't been able to get ahold of my dad all day. Something big is going on, but I don't know what."

"Is it the alpha challenge?" I whisper, scared to say it out loud. I don't want it to be true.

Her entire face pales. "You don't think, do you?"

"Mateo still isn't here?" The sound of Levi's voice makes me jump. He's so sneaky.

I turn around, putting my hand to my heart. "You scared me."

He smirks. "Sorry. I figured since Mateo isn't here, I'd come to class with you today. We all made a pact to make sure you never went anywhere in the school alone after what happened."

I wasn't really worried.

Not in a room full of bear shifters.

"Hey, Levi." Zoey steps up beside me. "Do you know where my brother is?"

Levi shakes his head. "I wish I did."

"Me too." I lower my head. "I'm so worried about him. Do you think... that maybe it's the alpha challenge? Do you think Alpha George is here now?"

"No. If it was the alpha challenge, we would know. We would all know," Levi insists. "Especially you, Layla. Since the alpha fight is for you, you have to be present at the fight. It's part of the rules."

That equally terrifies me and makes me happy. On one hand, I really want to be there to support Mateo. I want to make sure he's okay. But watching him fight Alpha George is going to make me a nervous wreck.

"If it's not the alpha challenge, then what is it?" There is nothing else I can think of that would make Mateo miss an entire day of classes without telling us anything. He has to know that we're worried about him. And even Zoey says her mom can't get ahold of Alpha Scott. Something is definitely going on.

"I don't know." I can tell Levi's forcing a smile, he's trying to comfort me. But he's worried too. It's apparent by the way he keeps shifting his weight from one leg to the other.

Class begins. I notice that the teacher doesn't say anything about the fact that Levi is here. I guess everybody knows by now that I have four mates. And from the way his eyes soften when he looks at me, I'm guessing he knows what the panthers did to me.

Everybody knows.

But... they don't know everything. They have no idea that what happened was completely normal. Not just for me, but for other members of the pride too. I wasn't the only one abused. I was just abused the most. I was the easy target because I'm so small.

Class starts the same way it did last time, with a five mile run. I find the run is easier this time. And I *know* it's because I've been eating more food lately. My senses are getting stronger, I can run faster, and I feel stronger. I always *knew* I was under eating. I was eating a normal human diet. But I'm not human. And shifters need more calories to survive.

"You did much better." Zoey high fives me at the end of the five mile run.

I shrug. "I guess not being starved is good for the body."

She freezes. "Your pride starved you?"

I shrug, like it's not a big deal.

"Why do you think Mateo is wanting to do the alpha challenge so bad?" Levi asks. "Somebody has to get her away from the other panthers."

She nods. "I get it now. I mean, I got it after they beat you. But now... I really hope Mateo kills their alpha."

"He's going to try." Levi sighs.

# Issued challenge.

By the time dinner rolls around, I am beyond worried and am now terrified.

Mateo was gone before I woke up this morning, so I haven't seen him since last night. It's almost been twenty four hours, and I'm about ready to send out a rescue party to find him.

I don't know who I can ask about where he is. If his sister doesn't know, then who would? I'm certain she's already asked other bear shifters.

I push my spaghetti noodles around my plate, not really eating. I know Mateo would be mad if he knew I wasn't eating much tonight, but my appetite is gone. My stomach is in knots.

Out of the corner of my eye, I see somebody come into the dining hall. I look up, in hopes that it's Mateo, but instead I see one of the members of my pride walk in. They walk over and sit with the other panthers, who are all looking over at me.

Wow. If I thought they hated me before, it's nothing compared to how they feel now. I guess I can't blame them for hating me. It's my fault they lost ten members of the pride. It's because I was attacked. And my mates did what they had to.

"Mateo better win this alpha challenge." Tucker is staring toward my pride too. "I don't even know what they will do to Layla if he doesn't."

"I'll kill them all if I have to." Kai's eyes turn white as he says it, and I see a little ball of light appear in his hand.

My pride sees it too, and every one of them turns away from us. They're terrified of Kai, and I can't blame them. If Kai wasn't my mate, and if I didn't know he would die to protect me, I would be scared of him too. He's so powerful.

"I'm worried about Mateo." I twirl spaghetti around my fork, but I never lift it to take a bite.

"It looks like you're not going to have to worry for much longer." Levi nods to something behind me.

I turn around and watch Alpha Scott walk through a door into the dining hall. He came through a back way, and not the way students come in. His vision hones in on our table as he makes his way over.

"Alpha Scott." Tucker greets him with a respectful nod.

"Is Mateo okay?" I'll remember my manners later. For now, I need to know that my mate is okay.

Alpha Scott holds up a hand. "Mateo is fine. He's been with me all day. We've been... preparing."

Preparing.

"Preparing for the alpha challenge?" Kai asks.

I hold my breath while I wait for an answer.

Alpha Scott nods.

My chest sinks. Deep down, I think I knew something like that was going on, but I didn't want to think about it.

"Early this morning, Alpha George boarded a plane. When he landed here, Mateo issued the alpha challenge, and it is happening tonight at sundown." Alpha Scott looks toward me. "Layla, you are required by law to be there, and the rest of your mates are permitted to be there as well."

At least they can be there with me.

"There is something else," Alpha Scott says.

I freeze, looking at him.

Whatever this is, it's not going to be good.

"The law states that if Alpha George wins, there are no more challenges. You will forevermore be a member of the panther pride." His face is white as he says it.

"Then Mateo better win." Tucker growls out the words.

Alpha Scott nods. "Let's hope for Layla's and Mateo's sake that he does win. Because if he doesn't..."

Then not only will Mateo be dead, but I will too. I know that. Alpha George will kill me for what happened. And most likely, he will do it in front of the rest of my mates, because that's how Alpha George is. He likes to make sure that the collateral damage is as severe as it can possibly be.

I focus my gaze on Alpha Scott. "Maybe it would be best if Levi, Tucker, and Kai don't come tonight."

His eyes widen in surprise, and the rest of my mates start protesting.

I continue. "It's just... you know what Alpha George will do to me if he wins. And he won't wait. He will do it tonight. I don't want them to see that happen."

Alpha Scott shakes his head. "Layla, you know I can't do that. I won't do that to them."

"Just... if Alpha George wins, will you promise me you will get them out of there before it happens? I don't need them to see." I know it's a lot to ask of him. Because if Alpha George wins, it means that his son, his heir, will be dead. The last thing he should be worrying about is getting my mates out of there.

"It will be done." Alpha Scott reaches over and squeezes my shoulder.

"Can I see Mateo before the fight?" I ask, hopeful that I can talk to him, and maybe hug him.

"No, I'm sorry." He stands up. "Neither of the alphas are allowed to see who they are being challenged for before the fight. I know that it will be difficult, but have faith in Mateo. He is young and not as experienced, but he is strong. I have trained him since he was a cub. He is ready for this fight. And, to be frank, Mateo has a lot more at stake than Alpha George."

Alpha Scott turns and leaves us alone after that, and I push away my plate of spaghetti. There is no way that I can eat now. Mateo will just have to yell at me later for not eating dinner. But knowing what is ahead and what is at stake... I can't eat.

Nobody says anything as they finish up dinner. Even Tucker doesn't eat as much as he normally does.

The alpha challenge is really about to happen.

I just hope Mateo will be okay.

# The alpha challenge.

At sundown, Kai, Tucker, Levi, and I head off to watch Mateo fight Alpha George.

My stomach is in knots at the thought of what is about to go down, and my mind has played through a million different scenarios.

I do think Mateo is stronger than Alpha George. He may not be as experienced, but I think he will be able to hold his own. The main thing that I am worried about right now is cheating. Alpha George likes to cheat during fights.

During my eighteen years of being a member of the panther pride, I've seen about ten panthers challenge Alpha George for Alpha. And all ten times, Alpha George has not fought fair. It always *starts out* fair, but once the other person begins pulling ahead, that is when Alpha George cheats. And he kills his opponent without mercy.

I shake the thoughts from my head as we walk to the beach, where the challenge is being held. The sun is over the water, slowly going down. The sky is pink, purple, and orange. It's beautiful. And if tonight is the last sunset I see, I'm glad it is such a pretty one.

When we get to the beach, my eyes meet Mateo's. He's standing with Alpha Scott, who is talking to him about something. My heart races at the sight of him.

I want to run over to him so bad. I want to give him a hug. But I know I can't, and it kills me.

I hear a familiar laughter, so I glance over and see Alpha George glaring at me, but he's laughing. I imagine he's excited because he thinks he gets to kill two shifters tonight.

Hurting and killing are two of Alpha George's favorite things to do. He's not happy unless he's doing one or the other.

Kai squeezes my hand. "Don't look at him, Layla. He's not worth your time. Not anymore. After tonight, he won't be your alpha anymore."

God, I hope Kai is right. I don't want Alpha George to be my alpha anymore. I don't want anything to do with anybody from the panther pride. I just want to live my life with my mates. I want to be happy. And, most of all, I want to forget that I ever was a member of the panther pride.

A guy whistles, getting everybody's attention. I recognize the guy as Alpha Mutatio, the wolf alpha.

"An alpha challenge has been issued, and it has been answered," Alpha Mutatio says. "Tonight, Alpha Mateo will fight Alpha George for the right to have Layla Rosewood."

Eyes turn to me, but I keep my focus on Alpha Mutatio.

"Alpha Scott, Alpha Leo, and myself will be referees in this fight." He glances at Alpha George. "And I'd like to remind everybody that this is a fair fight. If the referees have to interfere, there will be consequences. This is a fight to the death, but if mercy is asked for, it *must* be given. But might I remind you, if you do ask for mercy, your spot as alpha will be stripped, because a true alpha never asks for mercy."

What?

That's horrible.

"Do both challengers agree to the rules set forth?"

"I do," Mateo says.

It's the first time I've heard his voice today, and my heart flutters.

I've missed him so much.

"I do." Alpha George has a smirk on his face, like he's excited about this fight.

I wish I could slap the smirk right off his face.

"Then let the match begin."

Before Alpha Mutatio finishes his sentence, Alpha George shifts into a panther and attacks. Before he can sink his claws into Mateo, Mateo steps to the side, shifting into his bear.

Alpha George seems surprised that Mateo dodged his attack, but he recovers quickly, leaping at Mateo again. This time, Mateo is waiting. The two of them claw at each other. Mateo take a big bite out of Alpha George, but it doesn't seem to slow the panther down at all.

I want to bury my face in Kai's shoulder. I want to look away from the fight that is happening. But I can't. I have to watch and make sure that Mateo is all right. I need him to win this fight.

Alpha George jumps onto Mateo's back. Mateo tries to shake him off, but Alpha George sinks his claws in deep. Mateo growls, and I know it's a growl of pain. My chest hurts, thinking about him hurting, but Alpha George hasn't won yet.

Mateo rolls over, pining Alpha George beneath him, but only for a moment. Alpha George moves quickly. He gets away and then stalks toward Mateo slowly, like a cat playing with his dinner. Mateo jumps toward the panther, but Alpha George moves out of the way before Mateo can pounce. While Mateo is distracted, Alpha George swipes at Mateo's side with his claws, tearing out a chunk of flesh.

I close my eyes for a second, hating the sight of his blood.

I need Mateo to win. Not for me, but for him. I need him to be okay.

I wish Mateo and I could trade places. I wish it were me fighting Alpha George and not him.

Mateo seems pissed that Alpha George tore a huge chunk of flesh from his side, so he runs at Alpha George, who is distracted. He's prancing around, proud of the victory that he's just made. So he doesn't notice that Mateo is gaining on him until it's too late. Mateo pins Alpha George to the ground and goes in for the kill. Before Mateo can do the killing blow, Alpha George shifts back into his human form.

There is something shiny in his hand, and he hits Mateo with it. Mateo growls as he falls over. His body shifts as he loses consciousness. Before Alpha George can attack him, Alpha Scott and Alpha Mutatio pin the panther alpha to the ground.

But I am watching Mateo, waiting for him to move. He's still breathing, but not deeply. Each breath is struggled.

Alpha Leo, the lion alpha, steps forward. "Because Alpha George has decided to cheat, he forfeits this round, making Mateo the winner. Alpha George will be sent before the council for a hearing about whether he is still fit to be alpha."

I run forward. The fight is over, so I can check on Mateo now.

"Mateo." I bend down, trying to wake him, but he is passed out.

The pack doctor rushes over and starts to check on Mateo.

"What happened?" I ask.

"Alpha George attacked Mateo with a silver knife." Alpha Scott bends over his son but leaves room for the doctor.

A *silver* knife?

I cover my mouth with my hands.

Oh, God. No.

Silver is deadly to shifters. All I can do is pray that the cut wasn't deep enough to kill him. I can't lose Mateo. Not now. I just found him.

Alpha George has his hands behind his back with silver binding. I look over as Alpha Mutatio and Alpha Leo start to drag him off. But Alpha George doesn't seem like he has a care in the world. He just has a smile on his face, like he thinks he's going to get out of the what he's gotten himself into.

"Watch your back, Layla Rosewood. Nobody leaves my pride and gets away with it." He laughs as the two alphas drag him away, but I turn my attention back to Mateo, who is still bleeding out on the ground.

"Is he going to be okay?" I ask, desperate to hear good news.

But nobody answers.

"Let's get him to my office," the doctor says.

Alpha Scott and Tucker help lift Mateo onto a gurney and carry him away from the beach. Kai, Levi, and I follow behind.

This isn't good.

# Something worth fighting for.

My mates take turns holding my hand while we wait for news on Mateo.

The doctor wouldn't let us into the office. He only let Alpha Scott stay in there with him as he got to work. I'm not sure what exactly is going on, but they've been in there for hours. Right now, I'm just trying to tell myself that no news is good news. He's still alive if they're still fighting.

Nobody comes out of the room until nearly two o'clock in the morning. I am the first to my feet. My mates, and Zoey, who was also waiting, all run over to where Alpha Scott is standing.

Alpha Scott looks horrible. He has dark circles under his eyes, and his face is pale. I'm sure I don't look any better.

"Mateo is going to be okay."

At his words, I sag in relief.

Thank God.

I don't know what I would do if Mateo wasn't okay. I can't even begin to imagine life without him.

"He is going to have a very long road of recovery, but he is going to survive. As you know, wounds made with silver take a long time to heal, so it could be a month before he's back to normal," Alpha Scott tells us.

"Can I see him?" I ask, hopeful.

Alpha Scott nods. "He's awake and asking for you. But only you. The doctor is keeping a close eye on him, and we don't want a bunch of people inside, just in case."

I nod, just glad I'm allowed to go in.

I walk past Alpha Scott and through the door to the room where Mateo has been for the last few hours.

Mateo looks... horrible.

His face is pale from the loss of blood, and he has a huge bandage on his torso that is red from the blood still oozing out. But he's going to be okay, and that is all that matters.

"Layla." His voice sounds so weak.

I stride over to his bed and grab his hand. "Mateo."

Tears fall down my cheeks at the sight of him. It's my fault that he's here.

"Hey, I'm okay." He squeezes my hand, but not very tight. He doesn't have a lot of strength right now.

"You did it," I say.

He grins. "I did. You don't have to worry about your old pride bothering you anymore."

I chew on my lip, deciding not to tell him what Alpha George said to me as they were dragging him away. I know that the alpha challenge is not the last we will hear from my old alpha and my old pride, but for now, I want Mateo to have this victory. He's earned it, and he deserves it.

"Thank you, Mateo. I can never repay you for what you did for me." I bend down and gently kiss him on the lips. Just a peck, because he is injured.

"If I would've known that an alpha challenge is what it would take to get you to kiss me, I would've challenged Alpha George a lot sooner." His lip turns up in the corner.

"I'm sorry I didn't kiss you before." I don't know what I was so afraid of with my mates. I should kiss them all. I should complete my mate bond with them all. "What you did for me was so brave."

"I'd do it a thousand times over. It was worth it."

My heart swells at his words.

I don't know how I got so lucky, but I have four of the best mates fate could possibly give me. I know I don't deserve them, but I promise myself to spend the rest of my life trying to become the mate they deserve.

I know that our fight isn't over, but for now I will relish in this victory.

For once in my life, I have something worth fighting for.

# The end.
# The Lost Girl, Book 2, is coming soon!

# Letter from Scarlett.

I've wanted to write a book at Shifter Academy again for a while. And I've also been wanting to write about different kinds of shifters being mated to one another. When I started writing this book, it was completely on a whim, but I actually grew to LOVE this story and these characters.

I did not intend for this to be a slow burn series. That one is completely my character's fault. I am so sorry. But don't worry, it will get there eventually.

I hope that you enjoy this world as much as I do, because I don't think I'll ever grow tired of writing about it!

If you did enjoy this book, it would mean a lot to me if you left a review wherever you picked this up.

For more information on this series, be sure to check out my blog https://scarletthaven.net!

Also, if you really like my books, join my Facebook group, The Haven. We just like to hang out, and have fun. Sometimes I give away advanced copies of my books, and sneak peeks of upcoming releases. https://www.facebook.com/groups/1899968653639439

—**Scarlett Haven**

# More books by Scarlett.

**Shifter Academy Series:**
**Different (Book 1)**
**Monster (Book 2)**
**Hybrid (Book 3)**
*This series is completed.

**After Spy Series:**
**Hacked (Book 1)**
*This is a stand alone series.

**East Raven Academy Series:**
**Ever After (Book 1)**
**Never Ever (Book 2)**
**Never Say Never (Book 3)**
**For Ever (Book 4)**
*This series is completed.

**The Spy Chronicles:**
**Finding Me (Book 1)**
**Keeping Me (Book 2)**
**Losing Me (Book 3)**
**Saving Me (Book 4)**
*This series is completed.

**Stand alone books:**
**The Bucket List: Famous Online**
**The Day My Life Began**

**Bayside Academy Series:**
**Gracie (Book 1)**
**Unraveling Gracie (Book 2)**
**Hating Gracie (Book 3)**
*This series is completed.

# Find me online.

**Website:** https://scarletthaven.net

**Twitter:** @Scarlett_Haven

**Facebook:**
https://www.facebook.com/AuthorScarlettHaven/

**Instagram:** @AuthorScarlettHaven

Printed in Poland
by Amazon Fulfillment
Poland Sp. z o.o., Wrocław